An Accidental Flatmate

Choosing Family
Book 5

Jennifer Raines

An Accidental Flatmate
Copyright © 2025 Jennifer Raines
All rights reserved.

ISBN (ebook) 978-1-964636-46-7
(print) 978-1-964636-47-4

Inkspell Publishing
207 Moonglow Circle #101
Murrells Inlet, SC 29576

Edited By Yezanira Venecia
Cover art By Emily's World By Design

DEDICATION

To Giovanni Battista, an Italian immigrant to Australia and my favourite uncle. You made me aware of whole other worlds, and I'll always be grateful.

JENNIFER RAINES

CHAPTER ONE

The lock clicked. Instant relief.

Casildo pushed open Anna Turner's temporarily vacant apartment door. Vacant being the only word that mattered. He stepped into the fully furnished, light-filled, central Sydney, with carpark, apartment belonging to his best friend Hunter's newly wedded wife.

"Thank you, Jaddatee." Cas believed blessings came from his dead grandma, so it seemed only fair to invoke her name.

Anna and Hunter had flown off to their honeymoon destination this morning. Cas hadn't planned to accept Hunter's offer to stay in Anna's apartment. In fact, he'd said *No thanks*. But circumstances and a plea from his older sister had made finding immediate accommodation urgent. He chuckled. Lucky Hunt had given him a key. Tonight he'd brought a hold-all with a few essentials. Tomorrow he'd collect the rest of his gear.

The apartment had been largely empty since Hunt and Anna's whirlwind romance meant Anna stayed mostly at Hunt's apartment, so the rich perfume of melted chocolate teasing his nostrils was unexpected. Amazing how scents could linger, or how the olfactory system could play tricks on you. Anna's go-to comfort drink was hot chocolate.

Cas ambled down the corridor, the scent growing stronger with each step.

At the loungeroom door, he stopped: Beatriz Gomez— but not Beatriz Gomez as he'd ever seen her in the five years since they'd met at an industry function. The scrupulously neat and professional advertising account manager always looked stylish—alluring, rather than conventionally beautiful—but tonight she'd curled up in the corner of a sofa in a multi-coloured, free-flowing, kaftan-type outfit. Her closed eyes and dreamy expression told him her earbuds blocked extraneous noise. Cas's arrival fell in the category of extraneous noise.

Her hands were wrapped around a cup. Hot chocolate. Good to know his sense of smell was still reliable. This version of Beatriz begged to be touched, cuddled really, but they'd never been on those sorts of terms. Cas had never thought of her in those terms. Until today.

Okay, I've had the occasional fantasy.

What guy with a pulse wouldn't? Beatriz was an appealing combination of lush curves, dark colouring, and charm, although her aura of "not available" had become a silent roar in the last few years. Happy couples, like Hunter and Anna, signalled "not available," but with Beatriz, he'd never heard a whisper of a boyfriend, girlfriend, lover. And they worked in a field where gossip spread faster than a new virus.

Given I'm not looking, not available works for me.

"Beatriz," he called.

No reaction. Not by a flicker of an eyelid did she register his presence. He grinned, although *her presence* was a problem. She was one of Anna's closest friends. Had she stopped by to check the place was secure, stayed for a hot drink? She looked remarkably settled for a casual drop-in.

He moved directly in front of her and raised his voice. "Beatriz."

Her eyes shot open, the hand holding her drink jerked,

upending the contents; she cried out and shot to her feet simultaneously. Her toenails were rainbow-coloured, as in one yellow, one green, one purple, and so on. He'd never be able to look at her regulation short boots the same way again.

"What the—" She tugged the earbuds from her ears.

"Sorry." He held his hands up in surrender.

"Is something wrong? Has something happened to Anna and Hunter?" Her expression leapfrogged shock and hurtled toward concern.

"As far as I know, they're flying off into the wide blue yonder, not a care in the world."

She was holding her stained, no-longer-floaty garment away from her torso, her forehead crinkling into a frown. "Then why did you break in?"

"I didn't break in." He held up his key. "Hunt offered the place to me."

She shook her head vigorously backward and forward. "Anna gave me first dibs."

"Ah!" Hunt hadn't mentioned alternative options for the apartment. To be honest, Cas hadn't asked if Hunter and Anna had offered the apartment to anyone else when Cas refused it. Just assumed it would be empty.

Her jaw set stubbornly. "So, you'd better go back where you came from."

"Can't."

"What do you mean, you can't? Anna told me you're staying with your parents."

Did you ask Anna about my living arrangements?

The idea started an interesting train of thought.

Here and now, Cas. Here and now.

"Technically speaking, I was on my parents' property, but my older sister Maha lent me her granny flat. She asked for it back, effective immediately." Actually, she'd begged him.

"Why immediately?"

"I don't ask my sister about her sex life."

Maha had looked slightly desperate after Saturday night's date with Antonio, the widowed father of two adolescents. Cas guessed, but hadn't asked outright, that Maha and Antonio had both filed romance in the too-hard basket years ago. Now, they wanted a little alone time to explore possibilities. Jaddatee's old flat—private entrance and hidden at the bottom of his parents' leafy garden—worked for a romantic tryst. Cas hadn't tested the possibilities in his six months' residence in his sister's home.

"It's not the first time she's asked. I can't say no to her again."

"Can't you go back to wherever you were staying before that?"

"No."

Cas had surrendered the lease on his rented apartment and moved the bulk of his worldly goods into storage when he'd handed every cent he could to his father. The Hariri family had found itself in the situation of being wealthy on paper and cash poor. Cas's entire savings, and then some, went into trying to save The Hariri building, the flagship of his father's company, from a hostile takeover.

In the end, Hunt had saved the building, but until Casildo's father finalised the sale of some commercial property in regional towns, refinanced and returned Cas's money, Cas's plans for his textiles design business and a new apartment were on pause.

Soon now.

"I need my own space," he added.

"That's not a reason. I was here first." She crossed her arms, and the damp fabric stuck to her midriff.

"Until we compare phone messages or can reach Hunt and Anna, we don't know who they asked first." Cas had been best friends with Hunter since childhood. His claim had to be stronger.

"If they asked you first, you must have said no for them to offer it to me." She used irrefutable logic, but the tilt of her head suggested doubt.

"Did *you* refuse?"

She stared at him out of stormy eyes. More chestnut than chocolate in colour, reflecting her intelligence and warmth. Beatriz's eyes deserved intensive study, dark and light at the same time.

In all the years he'd known her, he'd never just stared into her eyes. "It's rude to stare"—he'd absorbed that message before he was knee-high to his father. Not that it seemed to apply to the people who'd stared at his family.

Her gaze usually reflected endless serenity. "I've got this," it seemed to say. Today's mini mutiny revealed her as disarmingly human.

"Initially." She was uncomfortable with lying, an important quality in a friend. "But Anna gave me a key."

"Snap." Cas clicked his fingers. "So, I can't go back, and you should change into something dry before you do."

"I can't go home either." Her arms dropped to her sides. The kaftan stopped short of the floor and her toes peeped from beneath it. Cute toes on cute feet.

Irrelevant, Cas.

But the hint of desperation in her soft contralto stopped him. "Okay. I'm guessing you want to change."

She nodded.

"I'll make some more hot chocolate while you do, and then we can start this conversation again."

"Fine. But I'm not going." She walked around him and out the door.

He registered three things. At industry functions, Cas was aware of her competence. Today, she wore some delicate floral scent that emphasised her femininity. The apartment had two bedrooms. If she'd taken Anna's old bedroom, the second bedroom near the back of the apartment was free. And life might be about to get very interesting.

* * *

Beatriz cursed fate, Anna, Hunter, her parents, her sisters, and lastly, herself. She'd had a crush on Casildo Hariri since she'd first met him at a loud, crowded marketing industry function. A few weeks into her job, and he'd gone out of his way to make her feel welcome and included. He didn't jostle for attention, but had an innate authority, a sense of certainty about who and what he was.

A crush she'd ruthlessly wrestled into professional camaraderie, especially after her father's accident two years ago. Thank heavens they didn't work for the same company. Casildo in small doses was manageable. In his old jeans, washed-out sweater and hair, longer-than-usual, brushing his shoulders, he made her mouth water. He was more attractive than in his work outfit of chinos and linen shirts, more tempting even than he'd been in his tuxedo at Anna and Hunter's wedding.

She pulled her kaftan over her head and changed into jeans and a cardigan set. Work casual, rather than her lounge-about-around home clothes. Then she tugged on the socks and short boots she'd arrived in. Camouflage, but necessary camouflage for a conversation she had to win.

When she emerged from Anna's old bedroom, Casildo was in an armchair. His hair was tied back with some kind of leather thong, long enough to trail around the side of his neck.

Bea had told herself looking was allowable, lust was forbidden, especially since he'd never looked at, said, or touched her in any way remotely unprofessional. Friendly? Yes. Sleazy? No. Interested? Once upon a time she'd wished.

Right now he looked—chastened? Cautious?

Good.

He'd disturbed her peace. She'd been enjoying her new-found freedom, enjoying having a whole sofa to herself, rather than finding it full of sisters who'd become demanding witches while her back was turned, blaming her for losing a promotion she deserved.

Cas had cleaned up the mess and placed a fresh cup of hot chocolate on the table in front of the sofa where Bea had been sitting. Her irritation faded. "Thanks for cleaning up."

"My fault you had the spill."

He did that. Did menial tasks when other males insisted on their consequence. Yet, Casildo controlled final approval for artwork at the marketing company where he worked. Apparently, he had an "eye" for matching the mood to the product, for exquisite balance between colour and movement, for creating excitement.

How on earth do I convince him to go away?

"Can't you move into your parents' house?" Her first salvo.

"No."

He also had a reputation for easy-going politeness, no back-stabbing or messy office politics. Patient and endlessly reasonable, until you crossed a line. Or so she'd heard.

"From all accounts you love your family."

"Did Anna tell you that too?"

"In five years, Casildo, you've mentioned them fondly on various occasions."

A man who cared for his parents might understand Bea's sacrifices for hers, and by all accounts, Casildo cared for his parents. Unlike the last guy she'd semi-seriously dated. He'd ghosted her pretty darn fast after her father's accident.

"Okay. I respect and love them, but if I lived with them someone would die."

"Cramp your social life, would they?"

"I'm cramping Maha's social life by occupying her flat. She's got a bloke."

"Anna's boss, Antonio?"

"You probably knew before me," he growled, looking at the ceiling, before he seemed to reach a conclusion. "I moved back home for a specific reason. The situation has changed. Enough, so I'm superfluous at home, but I need a bit more time to organise a rental."

"I know what you earn." Bea blurted out the words, then scrambled to reclaim the upper hand. "After all, we work in the same industry."

Although, he hadn't actually said money was the issue with a rental.

I'm projecting because I can't begin to imagine that luxury. Not for two years, at least.

But questions ricocheted in her head. Back when she'd first met Casildo, someone had whispered that he came from wealth and mentioned an apartment in the residential part of the central business district, although he'd moved back home by the time Anna met Hunter. Anna had been vague about why—something about his father needing help.

Bea was intimate with the fear you breathed when a beloved parent was ill. Illness could bleed a family's bank accounts dry.

Casildo had moved home to help; she'd never left.

"Bully for you. I've got a rough idea what you earn, and you're sitting here telling me you want free rent enough to fight me for it," he said with a scowl, clearly unhappy he'd told her as much as he had.

To be fair, finding a decent rental at short notice in Sydney was like entering a bull ring unprotected. Bodies littered the arena.

"I didn't get the promotion. Jackson Smithers did." Bea revealed the name of the colleague who'd brought the situation at home to a head.

"Al'ama. He's a jerk. You're worth six of him. What idiot promoted him?" His defence was so unexpected; she almost dropped her cup a second time.

"Jackson's quick to announce other people's ideas and pretend innocence when challenged." Bea had thought Jackson's co-opting of other people's ideas was the result of enthusiasm, until she'd started to see a deliberate pattern.

"But you have no smoking gun."

"In an office where sharing ideas is part of the creative muscle, plagiarism is hard to prove. Plus, he takes advantage of being tall, white, and male to undermine harder-working men, women, and this daughter of Chilean refugees." She stumbled to a halt—she hadn't shared her suspicions with anyone.

"No positive discrimination in your workplace?"

"Only at entry level." She couldn't hide her indignation. "For promotion, we believe in a meritocracy. Funny what that delivers."

"Jackson stole your ideas." Casildo believed her, and relief rolled through her.

"Yes."

"Get another job."

"In the current climate, I'd have to take a pay cut to start over with someone else. Jackson has a mile-wide streak of meanness he hides from management. And I don't trust him not to gaslight me."

In her head, she'd already committed the extra income from her promotion to cover the upcoming increase in her parents' variable mortgage rate. Tomorrow, she'd be back to looking at ads for waitresses or bar staff.

"Jackson's won. What's his gripe with you?" He studied her, his assessment far too male, and she resisted the instinct to check that a button in a strategic location hadn't come undone. "Did you refuse to go to bed with him?"

"He didn't get that far," she snapped at the injustice of Jackson's vindictiveness. "For Pete's sake, I refused a drink with him."

"Let's rewind. What did missing out on a promotion have to do with you deciding to flee your family home?" His voice had dropped, deepened, and was mesmerising in its gentle encouragement. "Tell Uncle Cas all about it."

"You're not my uncle."

"But I am an uncle and a brother. I know how to keep secrets. There are three Hariri children, four when you include Hunt. We include Hunt. We adopted him. Unofficially. He arrived last. Two girls then me. Second sister married with two ankle-biters. I can get references."

"I saw you with them at Hunter and Anna's wedding. They were the flower children." They'd looked adorable. He'd been adorable with them.

"I've never seen them so excited." He settled back in the armchair, prepared to outwait her.

"My sisters were angry." Furious enough to blame Bea for not doing enough to win the promotion when she'd devoted hours to crafting a presentation Jackson had somehow seen in advance and stolen.

Fran, her youngest sister's exact words were, "*It's your job to support Mamá and Papá.*"

Neither of them had shown the slightest bit of sympathy, much less empathy while Bea's plans crumbled around her, and something inside Bea had snapped. Why just *her* job?

"I'm angry, and I'm not your nearest and dearest."

Bea never badmouthed her family, had thought nothing and no one could ever encourage her to voice the frustration that had grown from a niggle to a howl, but she'd never faced a dreamy-looking Casildo Hariri smiling sympathetically at her.

"They're angry because they had plans for the extra money."

He simply stared at her. "How old are they?" he finally asked.

"Eighteen and nearly twenty. They're at university."

And intent on living life to the fullest, experiencing all that university had to offer, unlike Bea, who'd attended classes and tutorials before taking every hospitality shift she could get.

"How many hours a week do they work?"

"They're looking for jobs." *Or so they said.*

"You're providing pocket money for your sisters."

He was matter-of-fact, not shocked or staring at her as if she'd lost her mind. Migrant families had complicated relationships in a new world; interweaving obligations that stretched across lifetimes. Although unlike her, Casildo had been born here.

"I'm working and living at home, so of course, I pay board to my parents and some of that trickles into my sisters' pockets."

Bea was happy with the explanation, part truth, part understatement of the century. And she had no intention of telling Casildo Hariri that as long as she was contributing to her parents' mortgage, key money for a rental apartment was a distant fantasy for her.

"Why are you still living at home?"

None of your business.

"Sorry, I shouldn't have asked that. But it looks like we both need a little respite from our families and don't have the ready cash to pay for it." He'd gone all serious and broody. His brood was sexy; her brood looked like she was straining to lay an egg.

"What are you suggesting?"

CHAPTER TWO

In his head, Cas tallied the facts and impressions he'd gleaned about Beatriz in the years since he'd met her. A hard worker, reliable, super calm, generous in sharing her knowledge and experience with her colleagues and, unusually in their circles, she wasn't a party girl. He liked that she was quiet, but not a mouse, genuine in an industry with a lot of show ponies.

Attractive qualities in a flatmate.

She attended the official functions but didn't spend her nights propping up bars or wining and dining with her girlfriends. Come to think of it, he hadn't heard her speak of any close friends apart from Anna. Like him, she hadn't brought a date to Anna and Hunter's wedding.

I was best man, so I had an excuse.

Admit it, bro. You haven't dated seriously for a few years.

Some betrayals, like being hunted for his family's wealth, tended to leave lasting scars. Although, with hindsight, he could admit he wasn't blameless, and that stuck in his craw. He should have called time before his last girlfriend Monique grew frustrated enough to want to punish him. Cas had disappointed his father. Again.

Bea hadn't been in the official wedding party and,

because he'd asked, he knew for a fact her invite had read *Beatriz Gomez and friend.*

Okay, I was curious. It wasn't personal. Just like I would have been about anyone joining our circle.

"First, give me a sense of your sisters' mood."

"Why?'

"Because I'm gathering facts."

Actually, I'm just plain curious about this side of you.

"Did you shout or just walk out?" He'd like to see her explode. Endless serenity was an impossibility. He knew because he worked at it. Clearly Bea buttoned down her emotions. Did she button down her dreams?

"I told them to look harder for a part-time job."

"Did they shout?"

"What's this obsession with shouting?" She crossed her arms defensively.

"You did." Cas pointed a finger at her, delighted.

"You want me to shout?"

"Not at me, because, hey, I'm innocent, but I'd say your sisters were due a blast. Did either one of them commiserate with you on missing out on a job you deserved?" Cas bet that hurt more than their selfishness about the money.

"Do you shout in your family?" she asked, obviously protective of her family even when they let her down.

He understood the feeling.

"Dad, Mum on occasion, my sisters, although not so much anymore. Hunt's not a shouter. I tend to withdraw a bit. To be honest, I'm not good at loud confrontations."

Because people were usually struggling with emotions or to communicate their frustrations or longing or worry. The one person he'd wanted to yell at was Hunter's father, an evil son-of-a-b, but Anna had usurped his role as lead protector in that area.

"Did Maha shout at you today? Is that why you're here?"

"Maha widened her big brown eyes and sighed deeply. I packed an overnight bag, and said I'd be back for the rest."

Cas had been catapulted back to an afternoon walking

home from school. He'd been about seven. Maha had begged him not to tell their parents she'd been taunted because of her name. *"Mum told me it means 'beautiful eyes' in Arabic. She'd be so hurt."* The first of many secrets he shared with Maha about slights, insults and bullying because their skin was a bit darker than most of their classmates in Anglo-Saxon Australia, because they shared whispers in a different language, and the food in their lunchboxes was unfamiliar.

"Are you always an obedient brother?"

"I'm a devoted brother." A role Cas took seriously. "Are you wondering if I'll be an obedient housemate?

"Papá's the only man I've ever lived with."

Did she just admit to no boyfriends? No relationships?

What twenty-something admitted that?

Even if it was true. Was it true?

Not your business, Cas.

Besides you don't need your own place to have sex.

"Something tells me your head's in the gutter. I'm talking cohabitation."

"Think of me as a brother."

No matter how hard he tried, Cas wouldn't be able to think of her as a sister, given she was a smart, self-possessed woman who turned out to have luscious toenails and who could throw a tantrum when the situation warranted it. He nursed that knowledge to himself, along with the image of her in a damp kaftan clinging to voluptuous curves. Not that he'd act on the attraction.

"I don't have a brother."

"Let's come at this from another angle." He was enjoying the debate, although he suspected, like him, she'd already worked out the only way either of them would get what they wanted—a respite from their families in rent-free accommodation—was to agree to share. "We know each other, we have mutual friends, and there are two *separate*"—he emphasised the word—"bedrooms in this unit. I'll let you have the bigger one."

"I've already got the bigger one."

"I worked that out." Cas smiled because she was smiling at him, and the curve to her wide mouth was irresistible. In a purely platonic way.

Work associates, her best friend is married to my adopted brother, who'll kill me if I upset his new wife, and—I'm planning to spend every waking hour and all my cash on a new business—no room for sexy games.

"How long were you planning to stay?" She heeled off her boots and tucked her feet underneath her, her body language signalling she was open to persuasion on the deal.

"I haven't decided. What about you?"

"When I left home, I thought I'd give my sisters a few hours—me a few hours—to calm down, then I unlocked the door, settled on the sofa, took my first mouthful of hot chocolate, and decided I needed a longer break. I'm staying the full month Anna is away."

"If I get the small bedroom, can I have that boxy little room the real estate agent calls a study as well?"

She inclined her head, probably trying to work out what he wanted it for. That was restricted information at this stage.

"Seems reasonable," she said.

"Seems like we can both do reasonable."

"No promises. Let's review how it's working in a week."

"Then what? We toss a coin to see who moves out?" Cas didn't want to move out in a week and was more interested by the minute in spending a bit of alone time with the private, intriguing, beguiling Beatriz Gomez. She was part of his inner circle now. It made sense to get to know her better.

Right! And the fact I've always found her subtle style sexy as hell has nothing to do with it.

Sexy, but unavailable.

"That's the deal. Take it or leave it."

"I'll take it," he said. "Do you cook?"

"Do you?" She shot bolt upright, and he laughed.

"Actually I have a few reliable dishes. If you don't like

those, when it's my turn, I'll spring for takeaway."

"What about tonight?"

"You haven't been shopping?" he asked.

"I was going to rummage in the freezer tonight. Anna said it was stocked."

"Bet she labels everything neatly. How about I get takeaway to celebrate our new living arrangements? Thai, Indian, Italian?" Okay, his budget could stretch to paying for takeaway for two, once in a while. And this was in the nature of a celebration.

"Turkish? I'm a big fan of Middle Eastern dips. There's a good place at the end of the block that Anna and I have used a few times."

"Works for me." Turkish was cheap. *Thank you, Jaddatee.* "I'll sort my gear then head off."

* * *

Barely an hour after she'd fled the office, Bea had fled her family home. She'd kept her mouth shut at work. The effort had apparently used up the last of her patience. She'd done a runner before saying things to her sisters she'd regret.

"You're lazy, selfish, self-indulgent cows" still hovered on the tip of her tongue.

Honesty compelled her to admit she'd probably contributed to their self-absorption as much as her parents. She'd taken on the role of surrogate parent while her parents worked all the hours they could. Her sisters had pigeon-holed her by turns as an indulgent or a stern adult, more disciplinarian than playful sibling, and always on-tap banker.

"Work is your life. It's all you've got." Lisa's, her second youngest sister, words had been a rusty blade gutting her, the truth and the lie in them equally hurtful. Earning money dominated her life, but she had other dreams.

Then Casildo and she had started negotiating terms, and somewhere in the conversation Bea accepted what her instinct was screaming. She wasn't going home until Anna returned from her honeymoon.

Moving into share housing is a normal rite of passage to adulthood.

Heaps of my university friends shared houses with strangers.

So far, I've only promised Casildo a week.

But a month. A month to do exactly what I want, when I want. Heaven.

I need to do this for me.

That didn't make calling her mother any easier. Her mother picked up so fast she must have been waiting for the call.

"¿Dónde estás?" Distress, more than anxiety, leaked through her mother's words.

"I'm at Anna's apartment. It's empty"—or it had been when she'd arrived, shocks were better broken into small pieces—"and Anna asked me to keep an eye on it."

Anna had asked her to move in, dangling the taste of freedom before her. Bea's gut-deep desire to accept had jolted her. Anticipating her mother's unhappiness, she'd refused.

"So you'll be home for dinner?" Straight for the jugular.

"No, Mamá. I've decided to stay for a few days."

Maybe longer.

She crossed her fingers behind her back, positive her mother could see what she was doing through the ether.

"Your sisters said you were angry. ¿Qué dijeron ellas?"

"I'm not going to repeat what they said, Mamá."

"I'm sorry they hurt you." Did her mother know what her sisters had said? They hadn't believed Beatriz would leave. Truth be told, they probably hadn't believed she had anywhere *to* go.

My fault for behaving like a doormat around them.

"They're adults, Mamá. They're the ones who should be sorry. Not you."

"You're right." Her mother's admission soothed the ache in her heart. Maybe Bea hadn't hid her growing anger with her younger sisters' selfishness as well as she'd thought.

"It won't hurt any of us to be apart for a while," Bea said.

"A while is longer than a few days." English might be her mother's second language, but she didn't miss a single subtlety. "I'm sorry about the promotion. You work so hard."

Bea didn't mind the hard work. Jackson's sneakiness and his sense of entitlement made her want to smash things. *He stole my work.* A little of her anger was reserved for the in-house convenor of the interview panel who hadn't recognised Bea's hand in the ideas Jackson had presented.

"I'll come by tomorrow and collect a few things. I might stay the full month Anna is away," she blurted out.

Anna planned to rent the apartment longer term because Hunter's place suited the couple better. Their race to the altar meant Anna hadn't had time to sort out her furniture and belongings.

"I'll tell Papá." That made it official.

"Thank you. And, Mamá, I've got more ideas to make money." *A return to hospitality shifts, maybe some freelance work.* "I'm housesitting for Anna, not paying rent."

"I'm not worried about the money." Her mother's regret slid into Bea and, in a strange way, strengthened her resolve to take this short break for herself. "I'm worried about you. You're a good girl. We've always depended on you." Her mother's voice dropped lower, so Bea was unsure, but it sounded like Mamá said "Too much. For too long."

"Te quiero, Mamá." *I love you.*

"I know you do. I'll be on my own here tomorrow morning around ten. Come then. Hasta luego." *Until then.* Her mother hadn't asked her to come home.

"I'll see you tomorrow."

Mamá didn't need to know Casildo was sharing the apartment with her. After all, it was a trial. In a week he could be gone. Or he might stay?

I might ask him to stay.

Butterflies started a series of frenetic Samba moves in

her stomach.

The doorbell brought Bea to the door of her room. She giggled when Casildo pushed the front door open far enough to peer around it.

"I'm back."

"I can see and hear that. You don't have to ring the bell." She leaned against the doorjamb.

"A precaution. Not sure how many changes of clothes you brought with you. Don't want you spilling more hot chocolate."

"I'm collecting clothes tomorrow."

He held up the carry bag. "Dinner. I bought beer."

"What if I don't drink beer?"

The smells coming from the bag reminded Bea she hadn't eaten since breakfast. Lunch had been a washout after she'd learned she'd missed out on the promotion. She hadn't joined Friday afternoon celebrations. Given her usual routine, that shouldn't be seen as sour grapes. She'd offered fulsome praise to the scheming Jackson Smithers, then headed home to—

"Bet Anna left wine and mineral water in the fridge. Plus hot chocolate. Not that I've ever seen you drink more than a few sips of white wine at all those cocktail parties, conferences and corporate gatherings our industry loves to host."

Bea had thought she was wallpaper to Casildo at those functions. Instead he'd watched her closely enough to spot her drinking, or rather non-drinking habits. "I enjoy an occasional beer."

"Great, I'll bring a couple through with the food. From memory, Anna keeps the table mats in the sideboard near the dining table."

"I drink from a glass, Casildo. I don't swig from a bottle." She followed him down the hall.

"Never doubted it." He was quick with the pickup.

"Good glasses are in the sideboard too."

"Were you planning on using a glass?"

"I'm housetrained."

Bea chose the best cutlery and plates from the sideboard. *What the hell!* She—maybe both of them—were celebrating a new-found freedom. Anna had inherited the crockery, most of the glasses and the sideboard from her maternal grandma. She'd inherited the deposit for this apartment as well. A small, older-style building with eight apartments. Anna liked the neighbourly vibe that came from owners managing their own building.

"I got baba ghanoush and hummus. Plus, you're in luck. They also had some muhammara from a wedding feast they'd catered." He set containers on the mats she'd placed in the centre of the table.

"I don't know that one."

"It's based on capsicum. Time-consuming to make, so not on the standard menu here in Australia. Do you want me to put everything out at once? I got some tabouli because you also go for the salady things at those work functions, plus a cheese pide."

"Serve it all, and I can nibble," she said.

He was more observant than she'd given him credit for. Generally observant, or was he interested in her? Her heart skipped a beat. What a fascinating thought when she'd tucked her crush in a drawer marked *Do not open* years ago.

"So, if you're going to pick up clothes tomorrow, you must have spoken to someone at home." He poured her a glass of beer then filled the second glass.

"I spoke to Mamá. Said I was looking after the place in Anna's absence."

"Mention me?"

"Your name didn't come up."

"Given that your mamá's never met me, it wouldn't. But she might be concerned about her baby girl living with a strange man."

She sampled the muhammara. "This is gorgeous. Are

you a strange man, Casildo?"

"Strange as in unknown to your family, not strange as in axe murderer."

"Good to know."

"But, as the son of a migrant family, which has unusually open-minded views on women's rights, I understand your parents might not share those views."

"I'm the eldest of five, twenty-eight years old." *And don't ask again why I'm still living at home.* Sydney house and rental prices made living on her own and helping her parents mutually exclusive. "Perhaps it's time I lived the life I want to live."

Lovely, hedonistic thought.

"There are five of you?" He wolf-whistled.

"Lucky I'm the only one who heard you, otherwise I'd have to cosh you. No, there are not five of me. There's one me"—she pointed toward herself—"and there are four other individual women with different hopes and dreams."

"It's them you're bankrolling?"

"I'm not bankrolling anyone." She didn't like telling him a half-truth. "Two are married and their finances are between themselves and their partners. I've already mentioned the two at home. Studying."

"You don't sound convinced," he said. "Bet you worked while you were a student and contributed to the family coffers."

"Do you contribute to the family coffers?" She waited.

He stared at her broodingly, then drained his beer.

"Don't want to answer? That makes two of us. Could you pass a slice of that pide, please?"

The habit of handing over most of her pay packet had come in her late teens. The habit of making sure she didn't add to her parents' load. Not a request, more a creeping awareness that her salary made her parents' lives easier. Two years ago, her father had been injured at work, upending all her parents' plans. He'd returned to part-time work, but it wasn't a solution. He needed to retire.

He wouldn't retire until the mortgage was cleared.

"My big girl. Help Mamá." The lullaby of her childhood. Bea had increased her payments.

Then had come the notice that payments on variable mortgages would increase starting next month. Her failure to win the promotion with its extra salary delayed her father's retirement.

At home, guilt about letting her parents down pressed hard against her chest. She had no answers for them, no answers for the rage, devastation and confusion swirling through her.

What the hell had happened in that interview room?

Did it even matter?

Space, she needed space to think, to breathe, and to come up with a new plan to pay off the mortgage in two years.

CHAPTER THREE

The sound of running water woke Bea the next morning, and she took a while to orient herself. Not one of her sisters, but Casildo. Lean, lanky, delectable-looking Casildo. He'd probably hate the description, but growing up in the expatriate Chilean community surrounded by machismo culture, Bea found Casildo's gentle strength enormously seductive. Especially when she'd guessed his Middle Eastern background had its own version of machismo.

In the last few months, she'd learned of his deep love and loyalty to his friend Hunter, a man he called brother. He also designed textiles. His unique wedding gift to Anna and Hunter of sheets, doona and cushion covers said he did. Was that why he wanted the boxy room? His equivalent of an artist's garret? Would he tell her if she asked?

Bea hadn't pictured him as a struggling artist. Those rumours she'd heard about money suggested not just that he came from money, but that he'd inherit a bit. One day.

He didn't act like a guy living on expectations. She refused to discuss her finances, and he had the same right to privacy. Money was one of those topics that got messy very fast.

People with money didn't always understand the

struggles of those without. Or maybe the superrich had different struggles. Another one of those pesky rumours said Casildo had been chased for money, or rather, his family's money. Anna hadn't said anything, but then Anna had had less to do with Casildo than Bea over the years. It wasn't until Anna met Hunter that she'd spent more time with Casildo. Anna liked him, mostly because of his absolute loyalty to Hunter.

Not dating, and not discussing her promise to her parents made life simpler.

I'm not dating Casildo.

I'm not thinking of dating anyone, much less Casildo.

We both work. We have friends in common. Friends we want to keep.

I've given him a week's trial as a housemate. Not much can happen in a week.

* * *

Cas had set his alarm for early. In and out of the shower before Beatriz stirred, a habit he'd learned living with two sisters. Five daughters. He pictured steamy bathrooms, barely-there lingerie draped over clotheslines. Multi-coloured? There'd been a kid in his class who was the sixth son. Each son had been assigned a colour, so clothes couldn't be confused or misclaimed. Wow!

Does the Gomez household have a timetable for showers?

Will she tell me if I ask? Or look at me as if I'm a sexist idiot again?

It's a logistical issue, a real question. Bet her parents thought about it.

Beatriz and he had each needed an immediate bolthole. Both of them had chosen Anna's apartment because it was rent free. For a finite period. But Cas planned to have his new business premises lined up by the end of this month. He could bunk down there for a bit if need be, or see if Hunt knew someone with a room free. Serving Beatriz breakfast was his opening bid in convincing her she could tolerate him for more than a week.

"Coffee, tea, more hot chocolate?" Cas asked.

She was back in her neat jeans and cardigan this morning. Her limited wardrobe confirmed her story that she'd got as far as snatching a few hours of freedom. He'd regret disrupting her plans, except she intrigued him. She'd always intrigued him. She was so self-contained, so unflappable, when his gut told him she had more layers than a black forest cake. He had a secret addiction to black forest cake. Chocolate, cherries, whipped cream and Beatriz made for a delicious fantasy. Instinct told him she'd forced her nicely rounded self into a square hole, and he was the lucky witness to her breaking out.

"Anything without caffeine?"

"You can't start the day without caffeine."

Even her clothes intrigued Cas. Good quality, sustainable fabrics, classic designs that she was comfortable wearing more than once. Her choice wasn't dictated by a budget, or only partly. He'd seen her hand glide over a sofa or a drape, testing the fabric, making a tactile connection. Last night's kaftan was a tie dye cotton, possibly even second-hand because he could have sworn it was an authentic Malaysian design.

She looked down her pert nose, and stepped around him to check the cupboard. "Three ginger tea works."

"For what?"

"If you're going to question every food or drink choice I make this"—she made a circling gesture with her hand—"cohabiting won't work."

"We agreed on Turkish and beer last night." He moved out of her way. "I picked up some fruit at the same time, if you're prepared to poison your gloriously healthy body with oranges or bananas?"

"I'll shop later." She filled a teapot with boiling water; a gallon at least of the gingers.

"*We'll* shop later. I have a car. We'll need a few supplies."

"I'm meeting Mamá this morning and collecting more clothes." She carried her pot to the table.

"What about food? An army runs on its stomach."

"'You can't start the day without caffeine', 'An army runs on its stomach'—do you always talk in clichés?"

"Just establishing your routine. I'd say grumpy until you've downed your ginger pick-me-up."

She drummed her nails on the table. "I'm nervous. I've made up my mind that I'm staying, but I'm nervous. Mamá will feel she's let me down in some way. She'll have food, and she'll smile, but I'm afraid I've hurt her."

Cas took the seat beside her and leaned against her upper arm. "My mother cried the first time I moved out. I felt like a traitor. She told me to go, while the tears poured down her cheeks. Leaving home is complicated, but it's a normal rite of passage."

"My sisters lived at home until they married."

"Lucky them," he muttered. Was she breaking some sort of religious or cultural taboo? "It's different for everyone. Want me to take you over there?"

Her sisters had hurt her, taken her hard work for granted, and she worried about taking something for herself. Marshmallow soft and hiding it behind scratchiness. Cas had seen the same confusion in the children of other migrant families. Often, it was the eldest girl expected to make the most sacrifices from early childhood. Maha's interest in childcare had been partly honed by looking after him and his other sister Zahra from before Maha turned ten.

"Better not. I could be there a while."

Not a complete no.

"Then text me when you're ready to leave, and I'll come and get you."

"How do I explain you?"

Cas grimaced. "Am I going to be your dirty little secret?"

"*Our* secret. For a while. Mamá and Papá need time to adjust to me moving out. Moving out for a few weeks."

So, she intended to go back.

"But, I wouldn't have agreed to let you stay if I didn't trust you."

"Let me stay!" He pretended outrage to hide the kick of pleasure discovering the lovely Beatriz Gomez trusted him to share an apartment with her. For a week. She was careful about boundaries.

He'd never lived with a woman, apart from his mother and sisters. Girlfriends had stayed over, or he'd stayed at theirs for shorter or longer periods. Most of them got sick of his long work hours and reluctance to party. His fault, and when he'd started spending less and less time with Monique, she'd probably felt entitled to target his family's money.

He still woke in a sweat some nights reliving those weeks when he'd cursed his naivety. The devastation in his father's eyes showed Cas had fallen short. Again. You'd think he'd have learned from Hunter's experiences. Instead, his obsession with establishing his own textile and fabric design business had made him an easy target.

I'm carrying your child.

Not true, but he'd run out of options, until Hunt and Maha had stepped in.

Avoiding commitment had been his takeaway, especially now he was about to devote every waking moment to his new business.

Cas pulled into the driveway of the neat two-story home in Artarmon. Not a suburb he knew well, but colleagues talked about property—*my family talks property*. Artarmon had shot up the charts in recent years because of its proximity to transport and good schools. Worth a bit, when he'd assumed the family was struggling. An assumption based on his assumption Beatriz was still living at home, so her board money supplemented the family's budget.

Maybe Beatriz was hiding a secret addiction or saving for a dream? That would also explain staying at home.

What's your dream, Beatriz?

She must have been watching for him, because the front door was thrown wide when he pulled up. Beatriz trundled a large suitcase up the path, a mature woman with a food carry bag behind her. The resemblance was strong. Beatriz would age like her mother, some grey in the thick dark waves, a few wrinkles, still beautiful, much like his own mother, lines of laughter and love for the most part, but no families escaped tragedies.

"Hello, Beatriz, Mrs. Gomez." He popped the boot and loaded the suitcase, sliding it in beside the boxes he'd collected this morning.

"Casildo Hariri, isn't it?" Mrs. Gomez stretched out a hand, her smile warm. "I saw your face in some of Anna's wedding photos."

Saw his face and was interested enough to ask who he was? Or had Beatriz mentioned him positively?

"I was best man. I've known Hunter since we were kids." He flashed his most innocent smile.

"It's good of you to help Beatriz move in."

"Anna would shred me if I didn't help a friend of hers."

He was paranoid or burdened with a guilty conscience if he thought every sentence coming out of Mrs. Gomez's bow-shaped mouth was loaded.

"They're on their honeymoon, aren't they?"

"A secret location for a month," Cas volunteered. "They promised to send us occasional proof of life shots, but so far I haven't heard a word. What about you, Beatriz?"

"Nothing yet, but it hasn't been forty-eight hours."

"And Anna wanted Beatriz to look after her apartment. That's very generous of her?" Mrs. Gomez *was* digging.

"Anna thought the apartment would be safer with someone staying in it. She hasn't had time to move most of her belongings." Every word Cas uttered was the truth.

"Makes sense." Mrs. Gomez wasn't calling him a liar, but her delicate digging had sweat trickling down his spine. She only had to twist his arm behind his back for Cas to tell her everything she wanted to know down to the colour of Beatriz's toenails.

"Bye, Mamá. We shouldn't keep Casildo waiting. He's got a lot to do this afternoon." Beatriz hugged her mother, climbed into the car and accepted the carry bag.

Mrs. Gomez's bright gaze skated over the casserole dish on the back seat. The rich aromas of the recently cooked lasagne swirled around the car. Then Beatriz's mamá winked at him before stepping back. "No rest for the wicked."

Cas waited until they'd turned the corner and Mrs. Gomez was no longer visible in his rear-view mirror. "What did you tell her about me?"

"That you're a friend of Hunter and Anna's and offered to give me a lift. She asked if you were at the wedding. I said yes."

"Did she believe you?"

"I'm not in the habit of lying to Mamá."

"I didn't lie to her either, but I'm not sure she believed me." He jerked his head toward the back seat, while keeping his attention on the traffic. "She smelled the lasagne, I'm sure of it."

"When did having a lasagne become a crime?"

"What's in your bag?"

"Salady things." She used his term. "Mamá said it would cover dinner tonight."

"Bingo. Maha made the lasagne. We've both got food. That's the sort of thing that makes mothers curious."

"I thought you said you can cook."

"I can. Maha thanked me for leaving her place neat."

"Do you need a thank you for leaving a place neat?" Her stare was boring a hole right through his temple.

"I was born neat, or at least had neatness bred into me by the time I hit adolescence. Maha was saying a whole lot of complicated things, but mostly she was saying she loves me, and while she kicked me out, she'll always have my back."

"You're close."

"We're a close family. Hunt's part of that. Now Anna. As a friend of Anna's, we'd look favourably on letting you join too." Cas winked at her.

"Thanks, but I've got my hands full with the family I've got." Her hands sat neatly on the carry bag in her lap in contrast to what he guessed was her muddled mind. Moving out was both terrifying and hopeful.

"Your mum's got a good memory if she recognised me from the wedding photos."

"Mamá loves weddings; she pays attention to the minutest details. You were front and centre in a few, so she asked your name and how you were connected to Hunter."

***

Mamá had tunnel vision where good-looking men in the vicinity of any of her daughters was concerned. Pity she hadn't twigged that Bea avoided dating because the vaguest reference to her financial commitments to her family turned most of those charming, attentive men into affronted cockerels, lowering their heads and strutting in front of her declaring they were in no position to support her while she supported her family.

Not that she asked. Ever.

But the scars from those encounters were still raw. What did those would-be lovers see when they looked at her? What did her sisters see? A reliable bank? Certainly not a flesh-and-blood woman with wants and needs.

"My mum doesn't talk about weddings. Maha sat on her and tickled her until Mum promised she'd never so much as say 'Are you dating so and so?'"

"Wow. That's unusual in your culture, isn't it?"

"Mum and Dad emigrated after Maha was born. They wanted her to have the same opportunities and freedoms as a son would, and figured that would be harder in Saudi Arabia than here. They're also non-believers, and being a non-believer is a crime."

"You mean they're not practising Muslims?" Bea hadn't considered Casildo's faith. Her own was shaky despite Catholic parents.

"Yeah, didn't stop some people labelling us as terrorists when I was a kid."

"What about grandparents? Did a granny ever live in that granny flat?" Bea had weathered taunts about her immigrant status at school, but attending a local Catholic school had muted the worst.

"Mum's mum—Jaddatee—came with them. Her husband died about a year earlier. She was a devout Muslim. Mum was worried about how Jaddatee would be treated when her oldest daughter ran away from the country. Why did your parents come to Australia?"

That tattle-tale at work had emphasised Casildo was the only son and assumed he'd inherit the bulk of his family's wealth. This was the first time she'd heard him talk in specifics about his family, and it didn't sound like a traditional Arabic family where an only son might be treated like a minor deity.

"Opportunity, more for us kids than themselves. They both had to settle for jobs below their qualification level. 'We sacrificed a lot so you could have this opportunity.' And now I sound like I'm whining." Bea was tired and, not for the first time, aware she was lonely.

"You are whining. They did sacrifice a lot. But you're allowed to have other dreams. What are your dreams, Beatriz?"

His gentle rumble was seductive, irresistible bait to a sister who'd begun to hide in the shadows of her home, and to a professional who was overlooked for a slick newcomer at work. Reliable, but no one's first choice.

"When I grow up"—she mocked herself—"I want to work for myself, have one or two clients I can focus on, provide the full gamut of services from branding to marketing and financial management."

"Does your family know?" He pulled up in Anna's car

park and turned to face her.

"Does your family know your dreams?" She turned the question back on him.

"Dreams change when times change. But yes, I've talked about my dreams in the past."

He'd carried a light inside him, a fanciful concept, but Bea had been drawn to that light, to the joy it represented when she'd first met him. His comment flicked a switch, and the light dimmed. "But you won't tell me?"

His exclusion stung.

"For no good reason, I'm not telling anyone yet." He paused, then sent her a rueful smile. "That's not an answer. The truth is, I don't want to jinx them. Sooo ... back to your dreams."

"I'm supposed to share, but you won't."

"Seems unfair, I know." He sounded genuinely sorry. "I'll tell you when I can."

"I need my head read because I believe you," she said.

"To recap, you're imposing on the generous hospitality of our mutual friends because you're seriously peeved at your sisters and planning rebellion."

"Moving here is the nature of guns across the bows."

I will not be a doormat for my sisters.

Bea was laying the groundwork for a declaration that she'd continue with mortgage payments, but she was through providing her sisters with an allowance.

"Rebellion should include blasting people from their complacency."

"Is that what you're planning?"

"Absolutely. Maybe you can add the lasagne to your first load upstairs. I'll bring up your bag." Conversation closed. What did rebellion look like for Casildo Hariri?

Why are you afraid of jinxing your dreams if you talk about them?
I made mine sound flippant in response.

That's because I can't imagine enough free space to make mine happen.

Bea propped the front door open, then put the food in

the fridge. Casildo had left her suitcase inside the door. She rolled it into her room, then started back downstairs. He was already at the first landing. "I'll help with the boxes."

"No need," he said.

She ignored him and continued down. The boxes weren't large, but the first one was unexpectedly heavy. She passed Casildo on her way back upstairs.

"Thanks, but I'll be right," he repeated.

She stuck her head in the second bedroom, then the smaller room. His box sat on the floor beside a desk. She stacked hers on top, and headed back down the stairs. Casildo had two boxes this time.

"There's only one small one left." Casildo passed her at a run.

"Great." This had turned into some bizarre competition. "You picked me up. I can help shift a few boxes in return."

He grunted.

She hoisted the final box onto her hip, shut the boot, and turned toward the apartment. Casildo took the steps two at a time, reaching her side and stretching out his hands for the box. She fumbled, or he fumbled, and the box fell to the ground, the contents spilling over the pavement.

"Al'ama," he muttered.

"What does that mean?"

"Damn."

"I can do better than that. Hell, bloody hell, perishing hell."

He dropped to his haunches. "It's fine. I'll pick them up."

"What's your problem?" she asked. "We'll pick them up. Unless you've got a secret stash of porn under those brown paper covers. In which case, our deal is off." She flipped a book open. "*Pitfalls in Commercial Property.*"

Bea's mind raced. His father was in property development. Hunter was in property development. Did Casildo plan to join them? Emulate them? Her mind instantly rejected the idea.

You'd hate it.

"Obviously not porn." He grabbed the book from her. Then bent, straightened the box and stacked books on top of each other.

"It might as well be." Bea snatched the last one from the ground and pressed it into his chest. "What's going on, Casildo?"

"Not that it's any of your business, but I'm doing some research." He hoisted the box and stalked toward the apartment.

She scurried behind. "We'll talk about this upstairs."

"You sound like Maha."

"I'll take that as a compliment. You love Maha." Bea waited until they were inside the apartment with the door shut. "Commercial property?"

"It's my father's business."

"Which you have zero interest in."

"Not true."

"How long have you worked in design?"

"More than a decade."

"And you've suddenly got a yen to manage property when you could probably have joined your father straight from school."

His jaw set mulishly. "Leave it alone, Beatriz."

Bea put her hand on his forearm, registering a muscle jumping beneath her fingers. "Whatever's happening, this isn't the answer. Anna showed me the doona cover."

The design had showcased skill and humour, but also his perceptiveness in understanding what would delight Hunter and Anna. The fabric had invited Bea to crawl naked beneath the covers and wrap herself in its soft sumptuousness.

"Anna's a blabbermouth." He broke from her hold to continue down the hall. "What else did she tell you?"

Bea counted to ten before following him. She did this all the time. Mediated between warring parties. She wasn't usually one of them. "Anna showed me one of her most treasured wedding gifts. What are you worried she told me? That you're researching stuff you hate, or that you secretly design textiles? And if you weren't behaving like an idiot, you'd know Hunter wouldn't share your secrets with her. I credit him with more imagination when it comes to pillow talk."

"I'm sorry." He dumped the box on the desk.

"To me, to Hunter or to Anna?"

"Pax." He dragged a hand through his hair. "I don't do conflict."

"That's it? Fight over? You haven't shouted at me yet."

"Would you like a cup of that ginger tea?"

He had no idea how appealing he looked, annoyed at himself for losing his temper, more annoyed for badmouthing Anna, and capable of hauling it all in and being civil. Not blaming others for his temper tantrum. As tantrums went, it barely rated. If only Jackson Smithers had been within earshot, he might pick up a few hints on how to be a functioning adult.

"Despite it being before noon, a hot chocolate is in order. It's been a challenging morning."

"Did you know Hunter called it a liquid chocolate bar the first time he met Anna?

"And Anna described his coffee as inky evil," she replied.

"Wonder what they're doing?"

"Probably not squabbling about a few books," she muttered.

Although, Casildo Hariri had dropped some of his unflappable calm to reveal he was human and got pissed off at life sometimes. He just didn't spray abuse at everyone within reach. She knew that—on a professional level—but seeing him in action in an apartment they shared made it real.

"I'll get my hot chocolate. What about you?"

"I'll have an orange juice. Please."

She turned to go.

"I really am sorry. I go cross-eyed reading some of this stuff."

"Property development isn't your dream, Casildo. Art and design are your strengths. Witness your current job and your wedding present. Hard to be a genius at textile design and calculate how to turn a profit from bricks and mortar." She patted his arm a second time, this time adding a stroke to the pat, fighting the temptation to hug him.

In the space of twenty-four hours she'd learned he put Maha's happiness above his comfort and loved his father enough to take courses in a subject he hated, maybe to join a business that would keep the light out of his eyes. There'd been hints of this man in the Casildo she'd met over the years.

She added an extra half-spoon of hot chocolate mix to her mug, before zapping it in the microwave. Then she poured Casildo's juice, while reflecting that he'd been the first person to comfort her after her failed promotion. He'd shared her sense of injustice, solid reassurance that she wasn't imagining things. She placed the drinks on the table, and called him. "Juice in the kitchen."

"Thanks." A minute later he pulled out the chair opposite hers.

"Last point before I move on. Your bed linen design is stunning."

He stared at her for long moments, the expression on his face impossible to read.

"Is this changeover time? When you stop the ginger tea thing and switch to the hard stuff?" he asked.

Okaaay, moving right along.

"About ten o'clock. I sometimes have coffee in the café downstairs in our office building with a colleague. It's an informal meeting place."

"Have coffee with me on Monday at ten?"

"Why?"

Casildo turned heads. He'd turn heads in Bea's direction. *Do I want that?*

42

"A chance for you to unload after Smithers sidles up to you on arrival pretending to be friendly and gloats like the barbarian he is."

"I've never heard him called a barbarian before." Bea batted her eyelashes at Casildo over her cup.

"I spent a lot of time with my jaddatee as a kid. Even after I met Hunt and he broadened my vocabulary, I try to keep most of the cusses silent. Barbarian works—brutal, with an undercurrent of cruel."

"You've captured him perfectly. You'd be entering enemy territory."

"I'm modelling rebellion for you." His grin was pure mischief. Nothing remotely sexual about it, but her body missed that bit of the message. She'd never got over her crush.

CHAPTER FOUR

Walking to the café, Cas mulled over Saturday's conversation. Making a fuss over the boxes had been stupid. There'd been no way to hide the fact he was trying to understand business—when books were tumbled across the pavement. The saving grace, if there was one, was that the book she'd seen was on property development. Understanding the pros and cons of leasing property wasn't his major goal; he just needed enough info to operate. Maybe he should have listened to his father or Hunt more?

This way he could blindside them with an informed question next time they shared a meal.

As if?

Beatriz had leapt to the conclusion he was giving up his hobby like any sane person would. Although she'd seemed genuinely distressed on his behalf. He'd been tempted to tell her the truth, and it had been a long time since he'd shared his dreams with a girlfriend.

Separate those two words, Cas. She's a woman, and she's a friend.

The last six months had changed Casildo's calculations. When Nick Richardson had tried to financially kneecap Cas's father and Hunter, the ripples had spilled over to Anna and Hunter's relationship. The people Cas loved were under attack, so he'd handed over his savings to his father.

But, in the middle of that mess, he'd had an epiphany. After losing his business partner Mo, then Monique's betrayal, his momentum had started to slow. He'd lost sight of his dreams. He was increasingly successful with his current employer, so his family—his father—might have decided he'd abandoned his plans for a textile design business.

His family also regarded him as the one Hariri child who lacked a head for business, so he'd vowed that when his father was able to return his savings, Cas would establish his business on his terms. He didn't want to jinx himself before the money hit his bank account, so was keeping his plans to himself. He was assembling information—locations, venues, fabric printer suppliers etc. Only when he'd signed contracts and it was a done deal would he announce it to his family.

Beatriz had known about his secret passion and never raised it with him; called his work a treasured possession. Said his design was stunning.

She wasn't about to blab it to the world. He'd been selling designs for years, so was used to praise, but her instinctive support for his art produced a little buzz around the region of his heart. He could imagine her wrapped in a swath of his fabric. Unravelling her would be a delicious gift.

The flip side of Saturday's conversation was that Beatriz had agreed to this meet-up in the café. He got a kick out of being the only person aware that the oh-so-well-behaved Beatriz Gomez was planning more rebellion. Ironic that he wanted to help her with that, when he hated confrontations himself.

He spotted the café further down the block.

She'd wrangled a table in the window, so they'd be visible to passers-by plus any colleagues inside the shop. Smithers must have been a real pain in the proverbial this morning. Cas liked her new commitment to mutiny. He pushed through the door and paused. A deliberate second or two—he knew exactly where Beatriz was, but wanted others to notice his arrival. She raised a hand in welcome, and Cas strolled over.

"Hey, Beatriz. Thanks for coming." Impossible to read a specific meaning into that greeting. He touched her shoulder lightly, before taking a seat beside her.

"Did you take acting classes?"

"Binged on Bollywood movies in my teens. Did I overdo the pause in the doorway?"

She signalled a waitress. "I'd say you achieved your goal?"

"How was Jackson this morning?"

"Particularly barbaric. I like that"—a mischievous smile curved her mouth—"it's like having a special code. What are you having?"

"Fun." He laughed, then turned to the waitress. "A short black please."

"My usual," Beatriz said.

The waitress keyed in the order and moved to the next table. "What's your usual?"

"A flat white coffee, extra hot."

"Okay, I need more background. Why'd you want the job Smithers got?" While pretending to study at Hunter's apartment yesterday, Cas had considered her motivations. A promotion brought a pay rise, but he doubted money was her only objective.

Five years, Cas. She's never chased money, never cosied up to wealthy clients.

It's why I don't want to step back, when I have with every other woman I've met in recent years. Why I want to help her. Just help her.

"Isn't it obvious?"

"You're never obvious, Beatriz."

Slight colour crept up her cheeks. She needed to hear more compliments.

She wore simple black today, a long-sleeved cotton tee topping wide-legged linen pants. But she'd donned a waistcoat he hadn't seen before and guessed was of Thai design, hand-made in jewel colours that delighted the eye. She often wore the silver necklace; the interlocked links created a jigsaw effect. She was quietly stunning.

"It wasn't just the money," she answered.

The waitress served their coffees.

"Thanks, Dolly," said Bea.

"Thank you." Cas smiled.

"My pleasure." Dolly hovered awkwardly near the table until someone called her.

"That's some trick, Casildo. Reducing women to gooey puddles."

"Hunt told me years ago, I've got lucky genes."

She snorted.

"Are you trying to distract me from my question?" He added sugar to his black coffee.

"I want to get experience managing a larger team."

"From all accounts, your current team regularly sings your praises."

Her eyebrows lifted to her fringe.

"C'mon, you know our industry lives on gossip."

"I didn't think you listened," she said.

"Did you just pay me a compliment?" He grinned.

Beatriz was good for his ego.

Cas covered her free hand with his, absorbing the texture of her skin—like satin. Yet her hand slapping the textbook against his chest yesterday had revealed the strong backbone behind her softness. Her contrasts fascinated him.

"I may have called one or two people this morning. In the interests of suggesting that other agencies have noticed that you're a highly desirable employee."

"Careful." She stared pointedly at his hand. "Are you suggesting a personal or a professional interest?"

"I'm muddying the waters." He withdrew his hand—slowly, until two fingertips touched hers. "You want experience with a bigger team. So, you might be considering a move to another company to get that. Although moving to the opposition seems out of character. You're loyal.

Everyone knows you love TBR."

"A gal has a right to change her mind."

"Especially if she's overlooked for promotion in favour of a barbarian. A fairly recently arrived barbarian."

"I want to establish my own company. In time." She glanced over her shoulder to make sure no one was within earshot.

"You're looking conspiratorial, but I got that message Saturday, despite your attempt at flippancy." Cas hadn't sensed any last-chance desperado in her story. Her idea was sound, but it was a competitive market, and she'd need financial backup to start on her own, or at the very least some savings.

Hell, I'm absorbing some of the crap from those textbooks.

"You listened."

"Occupational hazard, when you work in an ideas factory," he said. "You listen, you try to work out what they're really saying, then you navigate an artistic outcome."

Beatriz's problem was different. This morning must have been worse than she'd anticipated, because the longing in her voice was stronger now.

"I'm ready for a new challenge."

"And your boss is feeding you more of the same?"

Overlooking her for promotion was inexplicable unless her boss had started taking her reliability and dedication for granted. Unforgivable in any relationship. The guy needed his head read, or someone to remind him that Beatriz was a very poachable employee.

"Yes."

"He might reconsider his position when news of this meeting gets out."

"Or he might think I'm being unnecessarily provocative by meeting you in a TBR patronised café."

Cas shrugged. "You're on a twenty-minute break." He walked his fingers back up to cover her hand again, craving the contact. "Your boss has been blind and disloyal. And we need to muddy the waters some more. Why don't you lean a bit further forward and kiss me?"

Cas hadn't planned this next step, but she'd been treated unfairly. She'd given TBR her energy, her creativity, her attention to detail and her loyalty, and they'd served up the same "Beatriz doesn't mind" crap as her selfish sisters. The longer he'd reflected on the problem yesterday, the more indignant he'd become.

"It's your idea. Why don't you?"

Was the very professional, unavailable Beatriz Gomez daring him?

"Fair point."

He tugged her hand, gently drawing her closer to him, leaned forward and brushed a kiss across her lips. Soft, but he'd expected the texture, so took more. Lush, and that had been his fear. That he'd start kissing her and be unable to stop.

Her nose nudged his, and he closed his eyes, so he could focus on the sensation of her, and found himself drowning in her unique scent. Her lips were warm, inviting him to surrender himself to the heat he'd find. If she opened her lips even a fraction, he'd find sumptuous.

Please open your lips.

She drew back from the precipice, and despite them being in a public place, he missed the connection. Her eyes were closed, so he couldn't read her reaction, whereas his heart was racing.

I'm in serious trouble.

"Muddy waters," she murmured, her voice soaked in coffee and shock.

Looking around, Cas saw glances hurriedly averted, but his interest in Beatriz Gomez, one of TBR's senior account managers had been noted. "Unfortunately, I have to go. I hope your day improves."

"I'm guessing Jackson Smithers's promotion won't be the first question people ask me for the rest of the day." She looked smug.

"Mission accomplished." He stood, stroked a finger

down her nose, before swooping to whisper in her ear, "I'll make dinner."

Her sensuous laugh hit his ears then his cock.

Casildo had to force himself to leave the café. Or to leave the café without her. In his head, he'd got halfway to an invitation to spend the rest of the day kissing her, touching her, unwrapping her from her lovely clothes. The little hum of pleasure she'd emitted, her closed eyes when she'd drawn back had sliced through him. That staring customer at the next table had startled him back to awareness of where they were, and his great plan for focusing Beatriz's work colleagues' attention on her. She wouldn't thank him for ravishing her in a public place. Maybe any place?

He knew in his gut passion was private to Beatriz.

I want to be the focus of her private passion.

I said I wouldn't go there.

With my current plans, it's not fair to go there.

Back at his office desk, Cas pulled a notebook toward him. Curves, with some sharp angles—nothing conventional. He didn't know enough to design bed linen for Beatriz, so he doodled. Geometric shapes—she wore those, also blocks of colour, then spirals. His mind swirled with designs his jaddatee had shown him.

Drawing helped him think. With a pattern taking shape, Cas figured out it was the fabrics as much as the designs that drew Beatriz. Touch was her medium. Fascinating. Maybe that's why he couldn't get the soft texture of her lips out his head. Soft, yet firm, seeking, yet giving. She tasted like every fantasy he'd ever had. His chinos tightened across his groin.

He groaned, setting aside his notebook to focus on the project brief in front of him.

***

Had that been his mission in invading Bea's work

domain? To shift her colleagues' focus from her failed promotion to what she and the friendly-to-all Casildo Hariri were doing sipping coffee, holding hands and locking lips in a public place. She searched her conscience and couldn't find a scrap of guilt. A gurgle of laughter built within her. She swallowed it, not wanting to tamper with the scene Casildo had created.

Hers wasn't the only gaze to follow him out the door. He was gorgeous. Not in terms of his looks, although he was drool-worthy, but in his desire to make her day easier. A lot of her colleagues would rate a kiss—with a promise of more—from Casildo above a work promotion any day. That's what his hooded eyelids and brooding expression had told everyone in the place. The sigh of envy when he left the café was audible.

She and Casildo weren't lovers, and weren't likely to be lovers.

The propinquity effect might be real, but the fact her best friend was married to his best friend/brother made any kind of casual fling a disaster waiting to happen.

"More importantly, I don't have the time," she whispered into the dregs of her coffee. "I have to find another way to make more money."

Why then did I kiss a colleague in what's essentially a workplace café?

I don't do that.

Neither does Cas, to my knowledge.

But Casildo had coaxed confidences from her she'd shared with few others—her desire to run her own business, to choose her clients. Returning to her office held no bogeymen. Casildo had neutralised Smithers as a gnat buzzing around her equilibrium. Casildo believed she was better than Smithers. His praise warmed her every bit as much as his kiss.

Kisses, because he'd come back for a second and a third. He'd tasted of coffee and teasing and shared secrets. She'd had to grip her hands tightly together to stop herself from reaching out to hold him in place. Keep him in place, tangle her hands in his too-long locks and keep his mouth on hers, slide her tongue between his lips. Pretend they were lovers sharing a kiss and anticipating more.

For magical seconds she'd forgotten her own name. She pressed a hand to her roiling belly. She still wasn't sure where she'd got the strength to draw back.

The whisper of his breath against her ear before he'd left had been another caress. Her body had shot signals in all directions saying *Yes, please.* She'd barely stifled her moan.

Inhaling deeply, she released the air trapped in her lungs on a conscious exhale. Yoga breathing to create calm. Not that she did yoga. Casildo's kisses were real and not real.

Hold on to the not real, Bea. He gave a bravura performance for a specific audience.

"I'll make dinner."

When was the last time a man, other than Papá at his beloved barbeque, had offered to cook her a meal? Her next in age sister's husband had, but he was a professional chef and had turned on a feast for the family.

If she'd expected living with Casildo to dilute her crush, she'd made a major miscalculation.

Bea heard his voice before she unlocked the front door. A bass baritone singing smoky blues while cooking a—? A curry, maybe Indian, if her nose was right in detecting garam masala.

"I'm back"—she stuck her head around the kitchen door—"I'll get changed and join you."

"Hi." Wearing a full-length apron that covered the front of his shirt and trousers, he waved a wooden spoon in the air, while concentrating on the pot in front of him.

The lure of the real swamped her. She wanted to insert herself between him and his stove and kiss him witless. Instead, she took herself to her bedroom and swapped her work gear for old jeans and a sweatshirt before returning to the kitchen.

"How was the rest of your day?" He turned to face her, his scrutiny serious.

"News of 'the kiss' arrived at the office before me." Her stomach did a slow somersault.

"How'd that play out?"

"You were scored."

"What? By people who didn't see us?" He held the spoon above the pot.

"I debated whether to tell you this because it's demeaning."

"Treating me like a body, not a person? Happens to women every day."

"No one should be treated as a set of body parts." *Or as a bank.*

"Preaching to the choir. How'd I score?"

"Some reports had you off the charts." She dropped onto a chair. "'Am I dating you? Are you trying to poach me?' Can I please, pretty please, introduce you to at least a dozen people, including Dolly the waitress?"

"Who calls their daughter Dolly?"

"Someone learning the English language? It might be better than Candy, from an old movie, or Fergus, which I was told came from an English dictionary of names dating back several centuries. Although my favourite is Choc-Wedge"—she held up a hand when he stared at her—"I do not lie. It came from a dope-fuelled haze.

"I was doubtful, but I have to admire your strategy. Jackson Smithers the Barbarian's successful promotion couldn't top the notoriously private Casildo Hariri's lingering kiss in a public place.

"Surprised you, didn't I?"

"Do I need to apologise to anyone?" Bea asked, hoping, for no good reason, that there was no one in his life right now except his new flatmate.

"Like who?"

"A girlfriend, maybe."

His reply was swift. "No."

"You broke your own rules for me, Casildo. Aren't you worried about blowback?"

The chance to unload on a willing listener was rare. She didn't join the competition to be heard at her family dinner table, although Mamá regularly came looking for her afterward with questions and sympathy.

"What did Smithers do?"

"Jackson didn't come near me after I got back, but Martin, my boss, hinted at a new opportunity for me. Suggested it was really touch-and-go whether Jackson or I got this current promotion."

"Do you believe him?"

"I believe Martin values me enough to make an effort, and I wasn't sure of that when I went to work this morning." Bea had responded early to pleas. *Help Mamá, help your sisters.* Not too many months ago she'd responded to Martin's request to help Jackson.

Look where that got me? Him trying to get into my pants and, when that failed, stealing my ideas.

"The more important issue is whether or not you value yourself." He turned back to the stove. "This will be ready in about thirty minutes. The spices need to meld."

"Want me to make rice?"

"Already sorted. Anna has a rice cooker. Bless her cotton socks."

"You're the only person I know who is probably serious when you say cotton socks."

"I asked. I've seen her curled up on the sofa at Hunt's. Cotton or hand-knitted wool. She buys them from an old woman she knows."

"I have a few pairs."

"Can you let me in on the secret of the mystery knitter's identity? Mum's starting to complain about cold feet in bed at night. Although she denies it when I ask. Woollen socks make great bed socks." He tipped cherry tomatoes into the pot.

Work functions didn't often invite personal conversations. Bea had seen more of Casildo since Anna and Hunter got together, but discovering this more private Casildo was a daily delight.

"Don't they have them at a department store? What about online?" She waited for his answer.

"Where's the intimacy in that? Knowing who knitted your socks lets you sleep better."

"You're crazy."

"You're not the first to that conclusion."

"I didn't mean it." She touched his elbow, wanting to erase the hurt from all the times he'd been mocked because he was different. She also loved that he loved his mother and wanted her to have warm feet.

"I know you didn't, but some do. Want to share a small bottle of beer while we wait for dinner?"

"Is this another trick question?"

"We can share one now, and share another over dinner. That's my limit. I'm working tonight." He lifted the apron over his head and set it aside.

"Is that what you were doing yesterday when you disappeared?"

"I promised Hunt I'd check his place occasionally."

He probably had, although given Hunter's apartment was above his office and his trusted PA, Donna, would watch the place as if it was her own, Casildo hadn't needed to do a bunk.

"Did you study property stuff all day?" Bea wanted to ask if he was okay?

"Not all day. Want to share that beer?"

"Sounds good."

"Go and get comfortable. I'll bring it through."

Since our café kiss, I'm reading double entendres into everything he says.

"Go and get comfortable."

"Do I slip into something slinky?"

Only if it's a natural fibre. She giggled.

"Do I spread myself full length on the couch and look inviting?"

"Would you prefer my hair in its current French pleat or tousled around my shoulders?"

She wasn't sure she did tousled. She released another giggle.

"What's so funny?" He put the beer on the table in front of the sofa and set down two glasses.

"Not funny. Fun. Thanks for this morning. And thanks for dinner. I feel much better than I did on Friday night, and a lot of that is down to you."

"My pleasure." He tipped his glass toward hers. "Is Smithers permanently neutralised as a threat?"

"I hope so." But Smithers's gaze on her had been speculative when she'd emerged from her boss's office. He'd been heading in to see Martin when Bea left for the day.

"So, tell me more about your dreams."

I've started having erotic dreams about you.

I will not say that out loud.

Madness to want you, because if even a fraction of those rumours about your wealthy heritage are true, if I tell you I need money, you'll smash the hundred metre record making your escape.

"Branding and marketing is a smallish but diverse market in Australia." She shared a more mundane but equally unachievable dream. "Some international companies and products just slide US or UK ads into the local scene, others want a specifically Australian ambience. But branding is broader than that. Political campaigns, promotion of ideas, managing professional and private reputations."

"Your voice is almost lyrical talking about that stuff." His smile was encouraging.

"Done well, it's beautiful in its way." She planned to be more than good.

"I'll take your word for it. Where's your niche?"

"I'm good at adding up the numbers, at cost-benefit analyses, at enhancing brand value. The projects I currently manage involve a mix of advertising and marketing, digital and traditional."

"And you make sure they run smoothly, within budget and achieve their potential?"

"I hope I do that." Sitting side by side on a sofa allowed for some interesting confessions. She couldn't see his eyes, but there was music in his voice. The barest hint of an accent, probably because he'd learned some Arabic. "Did your mother sing lullabies to you in Arabic?"

"My jaddatee more than my mum. How'd you guess?"

"I hear it sometimes in your voice." A mellow lilt encouraging confidences. Did he know that and use it as a weapon? Casildo wasn't a barbarian, but his fierce defence of Hunter made him a warrior. "I spoke Chilean Spanish as a child. I still have some. My sisters say I have an accent."

"Only with certain words and phrases." He'd noticed too. "What else do you want to do that you aren't currently doing?" His interest invited her to share.

"Advertising is about getting customers and sales. Marketing builds awareness of products and services. It's branding that's the key. Without a solid, reputable brand, your chances of longevity in business aren't great."

"So, company name, logo, taglines, fonts and colour schemes—the elements that identify your brand?"

"I'm not the artist. I'm interested in the values of a company or organisation. Customers buy into those and the emotions you stir. They build loyalty and repeat sales. I want to be able to pick who I work for, based on shared values, and build their brand bigger and better."

"You're an idealist."

"Maybe once upon a time. Now, I'm a pragmatist, and at the moment, I'm an employee who works with the companies and organisations I'm assigned to. With the advent of AI, I need to be agile as well as knowledgeable to remain employable and to find my niche."

"I meant it as a compliment. A lot of people in the industry know you deliver what you promise. That kind of credibility doesn't come overnight. It comes from being an outstanding employee whose consistent quality has helped build TBR's brand. Which makes it even stranger to me that TBR didn't give you the promotion."

"My boss hinted that the independent on the panel was vocal and insistent in support of Jackson."

"Which suggests the in-house staff were split." He was listening. He was a good listener. "I wonder why?"

"The independent was apparently very persuasive and the second in-house was chosen because she's from a different section of the organisation." Bea blew out a breath. "Now, tell me about the fabric you used for Hunter and Anna's doona, the dyes, the printing method. I suspect I could believe in those business values."

A buzzer sounded in the kitchen, interrupting their conversation.

"I have to get that." He pushed to his feet. "Maybe later."

If that was his dream, why was he keeping it a secret?

CHAPTER FIVE

By Wednesday night they had a comfortable rhythm. They'd watched two movies—*Die Hard* for Cas, and a bloodless French murder mystery set in Provence with subtitles and luscious scenery for her, and Cas had enjoyed both. When one of them cooked, the other cleaned up. Tonight, Beatriz had cooked.

"Are you off to your cave now?" she asked, lifting her head from a work journal when he ambled into the living room.

"Yeah. I need to do some work."

"Want me to bring you hot chocolate?" She never complained about being left to entertain herself.

"Better stick to coffee. I need to stay awake."

"I have that problem when I look at books on property development," she commiserated.

She had a point. Last night he'd flipped open a book at random. What were the odds? *Pitfalls of Property Development.* The book Beatriz had shoved at his chest on Saturday.

"*Ten common mistakes in property development and how to avoid them*?" she said. She must be physic. "I wanted to bin it."

"That was just one chapter."

"A favourite?"

"If I'm honest—"

"Please, be honest." She batted her eyelashes at him, and Cas surrendered.

"It opened at that page because I've abandoned it at that point so many times, I've warped the spine."

"So, what are the top no-nos for buying property?"

"You tell me," Cas said, wondering if she'd do any better than he had.

She tilted her head to one side. "Buying on a flood plain?"

"Got that one." And, clearly, he'd been right if Beatriz saw it as an issue.

"Buying a building riddled with white ants when the bank wants an instant return, or buying a property without checking the person actually owns it and is entitled to sell."

"Not bad. Apparently, it has to do with picking the wrong location, paying too high a price, or not checking council restrictions limiting you to eight floors when you need a fourteen-story building to double the investment."

"Having seen Hunter operate, I can't believe Hunter or your dad see increasing their bank balances as the only objective."

"You're good with numbers."

Beatriz was also exceptional at kissing, as he'd recently discovered, at asking questions, and about pointing out the gap—chasm ... endless void? between textile design and managing property.

"I'm not auditioning for a job as your accountant," she said, pushing herself out of her favourite spot on the sofa.

I already know she has a favourite spot and like seeing her curled up there.

She headed for the kitchen, and he followed.

I should tell her property investment isn't my goal.

But until he had the money in his hand, his plan was a fantasy, and he was superstitious enough to think voicing his dream would jinx him. He'd told Mo at university, but they'd planned to be partners, until Mo's father needed Mo more. He'd told Monique, but that had been a combustible mix of lust, and ego, and an attempt to explain his flagging interest. Monique's reaction was to kneecap him with her announcement they were expecting a baby.

"And you're brilliant at textile design." She kept saying that, and he always felt lighter for hearing it.

"Okay. I like textiles and fabrics."

She turned to him, the milk carton held against her chest.

"And design," he agreed.

"Let me guess, next step black satin sheets?" She was teasing him.

"I prefer to sleep on organic cotton or French linen sheets." He reached into the cupboard for cups. "French linen is really flax, and it isn't always sourced in France. I like natural dyes, so tend towards earth colours."

"You don't wear synthetic fibres," she stated, slipping a pod into the coffee machine for him.

"How do you know that?"

"We're sharing a flat. I see your laundry."

"But you missed the sheets?" He raised an eyebrow.

"I was teasing." She hip-bumped him.

"Guessed that." He rubbed the bottom of her waist-length Moomin shirt between his thumb and forefinger. "You don't wear synthetics either. At least not visibly. And no, I haven't snooped through your lingerie laundry."

"It's fairly plain." She dropped her chin, but Cas had caught the slight look of confusion in her gaze.

Easing her embarrassment, even at the expense of his, had him blurting out a memory he'd shared with no one. "You were wearing the jacket you wore yesterday the first time I saw you. I've seen it a few times over the years."

Her head lifted. "I wear most of my clothes lots of times. Me"—she pointed at herself—"queen of the budget."

"I call it your tiger jacket. Looks handmade, a vintage design with a grey base."

The garment's unexpectedness among the adamantly pushy marketing crowd had caught Cas's attention. What dreams did an admirer of tigers have? Thanks to their little misunderstanding over Anna's apartment, he had a better idea.

"It's got zebras as well and kantha embroidery. I wear it occasionally for casual functions."

"That first time was an outdoor event. Supposedly a spring fair, but there was a chilly breeze. It stood out. You stood out. You always do. I like what you wear, Beatriz. I like what it says about you as a person. I especially liked that soft, flowing kaftan you were wearing when I interrupted you that first night."

Her mouth curved in pleasure at his compliment. "I picked it up at a market."

"It looked like a traditional Malaysian design." He stepped back. Rather than keep stroking the fabric of her shirt, he'd rather be caressing Beatriz's skin. He had dreams about caressing her skin.

The coffee machine did its job, spat out a coffee, and the moment was broken. She handed him the mug.

"Back to the books." Cas gave a half smile.

Setting the coffee on his desk, he pulled up the document he'd been working through.

What's your budget?

What's the best location for your premises?

Proximity of your suppliers to the location? Buyers?

His father and Hunter could answer those questions without pausing for breath. They'd been assessing properties for years and probably already knew the prime location for Cas's business. Hunt had mentioned specific properties over the years, including shortly before Cas handed over his savings to his father. Another missed opportunity?

Raed Hariri had needed fast cash.

Deep in his stubborn soul, Cas had decided the fabric printing business had to be solely his. A down payment on the disappointment he'd caused his father with his declaration at ten years of age that he'd never join the family business, then again over the Monique episode. Giving his father cash was the least he could do, when he might have prevented the whole disaster if he'd been closer, if he'd been part of his father's business.

He wasn't making promises to the suppliers he'd been sounding out. Not yet. And he wouldn't, until the funds were in his bank account. Cas didn't ask for a date, had assumed his father's recent abstraction meant there was a hitch with settlement on the properties being sold. He'd wait, work more on his plans and be ready to act when his dad gave the all-clear.

He should have listened more. He'd ask questions next time he got the chance. "I bet Maha knows every single answer. Al'ama."

"Night, Casildo. I've finished in the bathroom."

Want me to rub moisturizer into your skin? Tuck you into bed?

What does the delectable Beatriz Gomez wear to bed?

Can I kiss you goodnight?

Get a grip. You've got three and a half more weeks sharing with her.

That's if she agrees to extend past next weekend. Maybe they could have a fling? Right, and pigs might fly. Firstly, he'd have to tell her why it could only be a brief affair. He only did brief affairs because until he established his own business, all his creative and emotional energy had to be directed to the business. Secondly, she'd probably geld him for his presumption, then Hunt would exile him for messing with Anna's friend.

Might be worth it.

"Did you say something?" She was outside his door.

Beatriz was good at numbers. He needed someone good with numbers. And branding and marketing. She wanted to launch her own business in time. Maybe, she'd help him—for a fee—a win-win for both of them.

"Night, Beatriz."

***

The intermittent rain on Thursday and Friday matched Bea's mood. Grey and soggy, she'd dodged downpours and avoided Casildo because, despite her head saying no, being around him made her body smoulder. Combustion was a real possibility. She'd touch him, and to hell with the consequences. And that was so unlike her cautious self.

But the taste of his kisses filled her head, leaving her famished for more.

She'd leapt at invitations for dinner from her married sisters, despite knowing she'd be cross-examined within an inch of her sanity.

A wind gust carrying a last dump of rain slammed the apartment foyer door shut behind her. She struggled up the stairs, raincoat dripping on the flagstones, the tip of the umbrella leaving a wet line behind her, her bag over one shoulder, while she clutched a food container to her chest. She glanced toward the apartment door.

"Coward," she chastised herself.

She'd gone out to avoid sitting across the dinner table from Casildo. Because she wanted to share a meal with him, talk about her day with him so much her brain ached. She wanted a sympathetic ear to listen to her vent against the financial responsibilities she'd taken on voluntarily.

Casildo continued to shower early. To have boiling water ready for her ginger tea each morning, to offer her a hot chocolate each night. He'd been in his office when she'd arrived home last night with the door open. There'd been no reason for locked doors when she'd tipped his stash of books all over the ground. He'd asked about her day, whether her boss had delivered on the new opportunity yet.

"*He's mulling options*," she'd said.

Tonight, she opened the front door and absorbed the calm. Casildo did that, created a sense of calm in spaces, like some mystic. His chair scraped against the floor before his face appeared at the office door.

"Want a hot chocolate?"

Does it involve us being naked?

"Join me?" she asked. Technically, it was their last night together. The decision was hers. She'd promised him an answer tomorrow.

"A break would be good."

"I'll meet you in the loungeroom." She headed for her bedroom, wanting to shed her wet clothes. "What about an affair?" she whispered to herself.

She'd had the occasional fling, one that had lasted a month, but they'd been earlier acts of defiance, when she'd been a student, when she'd done her first internship. She hadn't exactly been young and naïve, but she'd wanted to feel like a woman when for years she'd fulfilled the responsibilities of a woman—cooking, cleaning, child-rearing, helping the family budget. Recently she'd tried dating apps. She didn't regret those men, but the few times she'd ventured past kisses and wandering hands, the experience had been pleasant rather than mind-blowing.

Mind-blowing would be nice.

Making love to Casildo would be mind-blowing. Frazzled nerve endings …

A few simple kisses and desire has become a constant hum, thrumming beneath my skin—and that's new for me.

The smell of the chocolate hit her before she entered the lounge. "Decadence smells like a liquid chocolate bar." She curled up on the sofa, tucking her feet under her caftan.

"If only you could bottle it and sprinkle it on a billboard to double an ad's effect." He took an armchair opposite her.

"Don't mock. That'll be possible one day."

"Not mocking," he said, taking a sip of his drink. "Toying with ideas. Another occupational hazard. What else do you do when you want to be decadent?"

"As a kid, even as a teenager, sleeping in for even half an hour was my definition of decadence." Handling breakfast and getting her sisters out the door for school was hell.

"Now, Beatriz."

"Maybe this." She gestured with her arm. "A quiet room,

a friendly conversation and drinking hot chocolate I didn't make myself."

"Your fantasies are very modest."

My fantasies would have you heading for the hills.

"Your kaftan seems to have survived last Saturday's accident."

"It's copped a lot worse in its life, but it's a favourite. How was life in the trenches tonight?" She sensed he was doing battle with those books.

"I may finally have got my head around the connection between location, suppliers and customers."

"Does anything about property development excite you?"

His nose scrunched in concentration reminding her of her youngest sister with her hand caught in the biscuit jar at midnight.

"The annual architecture awards produce some exciting designs. Char House in Victoria has wonderful curves and uses charred red ironbark for its façade. It suits its environment. For city architecture, often the best they can do is sustainable materials and energy ratings."

She accepted the change of subject. "Do Hunter's designs excite you?"

"His apartment is brilliant. He remodelled the back of my parents' place a few years ago."

"Is there a role for design in property development?"

Didn't he understand how every misdirection he gave revealed how unsuitable he was for any role in managing property?

"There can be."

"Uh-huh."

"How was dinner tonight?" He changed direction again.

Why? Because he was unhappy about the future he was contemplating, or he wasn't prepared to share that part of his life with her? They both threw up barricades. She was keeping secrets. Inexplicable, really, when if she told him the truth, there'd be no more chance of kisses.

"Fine," she said. Not exactly correct. Conversation had

been more interrogation than a sisterly catch-up.

"Are you avoiding me?"

"No."

"You're not convincing me."

"My sisters invited me for dinner."

"More information, please. You have four."

"My married sisters. Camila last night, Daniela tonight."

"That sounds okay. I often eat at Zahra, my married sister's house." He had a family, a close family. He might have insights.

Bea lifted the mug of hot chocolate to her nose and inhaled, letting the aroma tease her before taking another mouthful. She rolled it around her tongue—rich, satisfying and comforting in the way being with Casildo was comforting. "Does she pump you?"

"About what?"

"Your innermost thoughts. Your secrets."

"Spanish Inquisition stuff?" He smiled, and just like that she was remembering his kiss. "You can say no."

"Lost that battle when I was about ten."

"Ah! They think you're a pushover." He abandoned his drink, switched to the sofa, and rested his hip against hers. "Practise on me."

"Practise what on you?" She'd lost her train of thought—hip, thigh, knee—his warm body pressed against hers, and her breath hitched.

"Saying no." He slipped an arm around her shoulders and cuddled her closer.

"What are you doing?" she croaked.

"Inviting you to say no, or not?"

"This isn't a game." But she'd picked up his scent, woody and warm—Casildo—and her pulse was racing because she'd just told a lie. She wanted to play with Casildo Hariri.

"Saying no to family is never a game." His brows furrowed, and he'd gone inside his head. Inside unhappy memories, and rescuing him from that abyss became essential.

Bea turned her face into his neck, nuzzling behind his ear, her pulse racing at her uncharacteristic boldness. "Maybe you should practise saying no to me."

"I'm not going to say no if you touch me." Whatever had troubled him was forgotten. His soulful eyes were deadly serious.

"You should." She licked suddenly dry lips. Was he attracted to her?

"Why?" His gaze settled on her mouth.

Did I invite that?

"Because my best friend's your brother's wife." She almost whispered.

"I've been telling myself that. At least a dozen times a day. It's not really their business."

"They care. They might worry."

"Even so, I'm not sure it works as a deterrent."

"Do it again. Semantic satiation—rapid, multiple repetitions can dull a message."

"In our industry, consistent messaging is the key to effective communication," he said, tracing a path from her forehead to the corner of her mouth with his index finger. "You're frowning."

"We want to remain friends."

"I can confidently say I'll always be your friend." He met her stare.

"That's a big call."

"We already are. We've exchanged more than words at all those meetings, cocktail parties and conferences we've both attended on behalf of our companies. You listen to people, you negotiate instead of bludgeoning, you want the best outcome for all concerned, not the one that makes you look best. You trusted me to move in for this week."

"I … "

"Speechless. That's rare. I like the way you do business. I get a kick out of watching your relationship with Anna. I'm already a fan."

"I can say no," she protested. She had a backbone. Just needed to use it more.

"Do you mean right this minute?" he asked, his thumb stroking her earlobe.

"I said no to Jackson Smithers."

"That doesn't count."

"Why?"

"Because he's a barbarian. You have to say no to people you care about."

"Have you ever?"

"On the little things, it doesn't matter. Will you swap turns washing up so I can study? Yes hurts neither of us. On the big things? I refused to let my jaddatee go out alone at the height of the anti-Islam backlash. Some idiots were pulling headscarves off women as a sign of how brave they were. She was scared but refused to be cowed into locking herself in the house."

"I refused to be pushed over tonight. In my own way. Tonight and last night. Two dinners because I didn't want to risk two sisters ganging up on me together, but they'd shared tactics."

"A few difficult questions, huh?" He was wearing socks, cotton probably. He leaned back and cool air pushed between them, leaving her bereft. He put his feet on the edge of the coffee table. "Anna gave me permission."

"I'll take your word for that. Tonight's sister, Daniela asked if I'd met someone. I said 'When do I have time to meet anyone?' Her husband came to my defence. He said, 'Bea knows nothing she tells you will remain confidential.'"

"Is she spying for the whole family?"

"Hard to know. She claimed she could be confidential. I didn't have to disagree, because her husband snorted and said I'd made the right call. I just said I was house minding for a finite period, reminded her of Anna's wedding, then shifted the topic to Dani's pregnancy."

"Are you envious she's married and having a baby before you?" he asked.

A perceptive question. Perceptive and brave. No one in her family had skated even close. They'd assumed she was envious. She was only envious that Daniela had found a man who adored her, faults and all.

"How to answer that?"

"Any way you like. 'Mind your own business,' 'I don't plan to have children because the world's a messy place,' 'Yes, I wish I'd met someone years ago and was happily settled in domestic bliss.'"

He would accept whatever answer she gave.

"Dani and Lucas are perfect for each other. He's with one of the big accounting firms, a rising star, and she took a job with a family law firm, mostly doing domestic law. They met at university and have been inseparable since. They waited until both of them were working, until they could support themselves without raiding the parental piggy bank. His parents have one." She swallowed the words "mine don't," but a smart man should guess. "A baby's the next logical step for them. They'll be terrific parents."

"And."

"I've never met someone I can't bear to live without. And that's partly down to me. I wear a kind of *I'm unavailable* sign around my neck. It suits me for now." There. She was being totally honest. Well, almost totally.

I've told him I'm unavailable, have chosen to be unavailable.

You're the first man to make me regret that decision.

"That's your criterion? Someone you can't bear to live without?" His voice held curiosity.

"What's yours?" She gave herself permission to ask the question, because they'd stumbled headlong into a very personal conversation.

"Maybe someone who can't bear to live without me." His face was in shadow, so it was impossible to read his mood. "Me, not my job, not my family's wealth, not my imagined inheritance—me."

Who made you feel unlovable?

A dangerous question, she wasn't brave enough to ask.

I can imagine not being able to live without Casildo Hariri.

In another world. Two years from now, when she wasn't helping to pay her parents' mortgage, when no one could say she was after his family's money. Then it would suit her to do a whole lot of things differently, like climb into his lap, steal kisses, and whisper naughty words, *tell him how he makes me feel hot and wet and desperate for his touch.*

"They're forecasting sunny weather for tomorrow." She drained her cup, wanting to banish the demons who'd joined them. "Want to come for a picnic in Centennial Park?"

"I thought I might be looking for new accommodation tomorrow."

"I think our week's trial has worked well. You don't snore." Heat rose up her throat.

Bea wanted him to stay. Actively wanted to share this apartment with him, rather than pretend to tolerate him because of a mix-up. That was what her visits to her sisters had proved. Rebellion was addictive—going for what you wanted was infectious and exhilarating.

"Have you been listening at walls?" He grinned.

"I have very sensitive hearing."

"Thank you. Is letting me stay another act of rebellion?"

"What if it is?"

I've admitted I'm not available.

He said we're friends.

Can I interest you in being friends with time-limited benefits, Mr Hariri?

"No issue. If it's providing me with accommodation," he said. "I'd like to stay. And I'd love to share a picnic. But I know somewhere closer. We can walk."

"Sounds good. My sister gave me some leftovers."

"Salady things?"

"My family knows I'm addicted to salady things. Although she tucked some roast chicken in as well." Enough for two meals, her sister had said. Or had her sister meant two people? "What did you eat tonight?"

"I defrosted Maha's leftover lasagne."

"We're letting our families feed us." She wouldn't feel guilty about it.

He shrugged. "It's part of how our families work."

She'd always put her family first. Would she ever come first for someone?

Bea had told him more than she'd planned tonight. Touched him, in response to his hug. Lying alone in bed, she relieved the moment. Hardly a passionate cuddle, but she'd trembled inside, and she'd invited him to stay.

Despite knowing she couldn't keep him, she was toying with more than rebellion.

CHAPTER SIX

Cas shouldered the backpack with their food and some cold water.

"I won't say no if you touch me."

I'm insane.

Cuddling on a couch with Beatriz didn't feel insane, tracing the length of her cheek, the outline of her earlobe. It felt natural, good, the first step toward something more.

Get a grip.

At least he'd had the sense to withdraw. He groaned as a different image entered his head.

"I can carry something."

"The rug." He jerked his chin in the direction of a tartan rug he'd folded across one of the kitchen chairs. "I keep it in the boot, in case I find a spot to stop for a while."

"When was the last time you used it?"

"An injured dog. Some idiot on a bike took a corner at speed and took out the dog. A kid came running, tears streaming down his cheeks at the sight of his battered pooch. I drove them home."

"That was kind." She folded the rug over her arm.

"Would you have abandoned a crying kid and an injured dog?"

"Probably not."

"I rest my case. Have you got a hat?"

"Anna left an old one in the bottom of her closet. Here it is." She plucked the hat off a rack near the door and jammed it on her head.

"It's back to front." He righted the hat for her, catching some of her flyaway hair in his fingers. He rubbed the skein—soft, silky—then pulled his hand back before sliding his fingers into the hair at the nape of her neck to test the texture there. And the heat. He bet she was warm everywhere.

He wanted to stroke his fingers down her cheek. Again. Cup her face for his kiss. *Again*. Their shared kisses in the café had made their cuddle on the sofa inevitable. His body ached for more.

Not gonna happen.

"Let's get going." Cas plonked his hat on his head.

Once on the street, he turned south, winding his way through the back streets of Glebe emerging fifteen minutes later on to the main road at the junction of Ross Street and Parramatta Road.

"Are you going to tell me where we're going?"

"The University Oval. I love this place. Loved it when I attended, love it still. It's an oasis between Glebe and Newtown. They have reputations as party suburbs or food centres or just interesting strips to walk down. But you know all that." He breathed deeply, anticipating the escape offered by a picnic blanket and a companion he'd never expected to have.

"Did Hunter study here?"

"Part-time, at night. In those days, he was working as a builder's labourer for his uncle. Sometimes, he'd come with me to see a game. Women's Rugby League was always a lure." Cas grinned at the memories.

"Is there a game on today?"

"There might be," he said. The traffic lights changed, giving them the go-to cross into the university grounds.

"The hill's a good spot, with a few snug places to prop your back and watch the game. Did you play a sport?"

"At school I did." She followed him a few hundred metres up the road, then detoured to take a place on the hill. "Now, I dance."

"Ballet? Modern?"

"Nothing formal. I love to dance. I make up the steps as I go along, or imitate moves from music clips or TV shows in my room."

"Can I watch?"

"That fact is not for sharing. Or viewing."

"Noted." He was tickled by the secret she'd just handed him. "Do you get all hot and sweaty?"

"The other night you wanted to know if I was angry. Now you want to know if I get all hot and sweaty. What's the obsession with extreme emotions?"

"Not extreme. I get the sense life has caged you into buttoned-down competence. That makes you an excellent colleague, and I'm guessing, an outstanding daughter, but it also leaves you vulnerable to the kind of attack Jackson Smithers launched." Cas could have said *to the kind of attack your sisters launched*, but he didn't want to hurt her, and he saw the beginnings of hurt in her eyes. "I'm all for encouraging your rebellious streak."

"What about *your* rebellious streak?"

"I've been indulging it for years."

And I'm about to go public with it. Use it or lose it.

He was about to use those hours of work, reveal his precious designs to the world and see what reaction he got.

"Convince me." She gave him her focused attention.

Bea's focused attention turned clients into lapdogs. Cas wasn't any more immune. She also invited the truth, because she was truthful. He'd never dated a woman he'd known for years. He was starting to see the appeal of graduating from friends to lovers. He'd been attracted to Beatriz when he'd first met her, but she'd disappeared for a while, and when she'd returned—he'd forgotten the timing until now—her unavailable sign had become the only signal she'd emitted.

"You mentioned my present to Hunter and Anna," he said. "It's my idea of a side hustle."

"It's worth more than a side hustle."

"Thanks." He'd started hoarding her compliments.

Focus, Cas, on all the reasons a relationship's a bad idea.

He started unloading the backpack.

When you start the business, you'll have no time or money for anything else. Anyone else. She'll be hurt.

I'd hate that.

"I'm looking at expanding it." And that was more than Cas had told anyone else. "Let's get this picnic started."

She studied him with her serious eyes. "I'd love to hear more when you're ready. What's on the sandwiches?"

"Salady things." He grinned. "And some chicken."

Two hours later, a new team was running onto the field. Cas rifled through the hamper to find it empty. "You ate everything," he accused.

"I had help. Now, I feel drunk on soft air and warm sun. Watching those women run up and down the field is making me sleepy." She yawned. "Doing nothing is completely hedonistic."

"What would you normally be doing?"

"Maybe cooking, maybe visiting family, maybe some research for a work project." She lounged back on her elbows.

"Here. You can use the backpack as a pillow. Or you can lean on me."

I did not just ask Beatriz Gomez to snuggle up against me.

He pushed the backpack behind his head, lay back and patted his stomach. Then waited.

"Ten minutes. No longer. Wake me up if I fall asleep." She was careful to face away from him, laying on her side, with her head resting more against his thigh than his stomach, but she was letting him feel her weight. Like the well-brought-up son he was, he folded his hands on his stomach.

"Now give a rebel yell," he muttered under his breath, frustration wrestling with reason in his head. She was a thoroughly nice woman, and sexy as hell. The first woman in a long time he could see not just in his bed, but in his life.

Pity my life is currently full.

Cas woke a short time later. She'd moved in her sleep, or he'd moved, until she was cuddled against his side, her head resting on his shoulder. They'd been felled, not so much by physical exhaustion as the weight of things beyond their control. Turning, he rested his cheek against her hair, inhaling the slight citrus scent of her shampoo. She fit against his side so perfectly he pressed a kiss to her hair.

"You didn't wake me." She spoke into his chest.

"The soft air and warm sun did for me too." He used his stomach muscles to lift them both upright, then removed the arm he'd tucked around her. "We should make a move."

"You probably have things you need to do," she said, looking anywhere but at him.

"I've been invited home for dinner tonight."

"Do you need an invitation?"

"No, but this is more formal. Why don't you come with me?"

Cas hadn't planned to invite her, but it felt right. He hadn't taken a woman home since he'd introduced Monique as his fiancée and told his parents she was pregnant. They'd handled the shock better than he had. Although, his father's disappointment was a wound that hadn't healed. But Cas was working on that, and introducing someone as lovely as Beatriz as a friend would ease some of the shame and guilt of taking Monique into his parents' home.

"And start more gossip?" Beatriz stared at him.

"The focus is going to be on Antonio and Maha. She told me she'd appreciate some support. You're easy to explain. We're old work colleagues. Mum and Dad met you at the wedding, and I introduced you as a work colleague, not just Anna's bestie. You're missing her, like I'm missing Hunt, so I offered you a family meal." The longer he considered it, the more he liked the idea. "You can distract them by talking about your family—five daughters—and living at home. Don't forget to say that."

"Don't push your luck. I won't lie."

"You do live at home. You're taking a brief sabbatical."

"You take a sabbatical from work."

"We both work at home." Cas bit his tongue to prevent him saying more. Her sheer pleasure in just doing nothing showed how rare a treat it was for her, and he got the benefit of seeing an unguarded, interesting and disarmingly sexy woman.

* * *

Treat it like any work function, Beatriz.

I smile, I nod, and I try and get people to talk about themselves. What interests them, what their passions are, how I can turn those into reality.

And I'm good at it. Casildo said so.

Casildo pulled onto the grass verge inside the front gate. Not for long, but long enough to provide an impressive view of the two-story house set among trees and a lavish, colour-drenched garden.

"Mum's the gardener," he said, without waiting for her question. "I learned colours from her."

"That's a lovely inheritance."

"It is, isn't it?" He swivelled toward her. "Thanks for coming tonight."

"To dilute the focus on Antonio?"

"I reckon he can look after himself. We're here for Maha." Another demonstration of his loyalty to family, another demonstration of the things they had in common. "Have you got your set of prepared questions ready?"

"For what?"

"For whom." He grinned. "For when the cross-examination gets heavy, for when there's an awkward silence."

"I can't imagine an awkward silence in your family."

"But Maha's brought a fella for dinner."

"I thought you said your mum never asked."

"Best to be prepared." He sounded serious. "I've already claimed the honeymoon question. You know, guess where Hunt and Anna are? I'll only use the baby question if things get desperate."

"What baby question?" she squawked.

"Guess how long before Hunt and Anna get pregnant?"

"It's none of our business."

"Are you claiming your family follows that rule?" He flicked a look in her direction. "Right. Babies are fair game if we're desperate. What have you got?" He drove slowly toward the house.

"Saying I'm one of five usually works as a distraction for a bit."

"Especially if you go through them one at a time."

"I could commiserate with Maha about the trials of being an older sister."

"Maha loved it. She's a born leader."

"So are you."

He turned briefly from the driveway to her. His expression revealed surprise and pleasure. He held a senior position at his workplace and was surprised she saw him as a leader? Was his self-doubt the natural questioning of an artist, or because as third child he'd always have been playing catchup?

"Just a different kind." She squeezed his thigh in encouragement.

"That might be the nicest thing you've ever said to me. Dad's my hero."

"Not Maha or Hunt?"

"You'd put Maha ahead of Hunt?" He frowned.

"Tough choice, but Maha strikes me as a fearless straight shooter. Although I've only met her at the wedding and a few of the pre-wedding gatherings, and she was smiling a lot. No serious topics came up. Anna's a big fan of her work."

"My sister is a straight shooter, so's Hunt. They tell me the truth, even when they know it'll hurt," he said, seemingly lost in thought. "I admire them as much as I love them."

"So, why your father?"

"He reminds me of some of those comic book gods you worship as a kid. Courageous, determined, sure of his path. He's both an inspiration and kind to his employees. He's also totally honest," he murmured, parking the car in front of the house.

"No wonder you're proud of him," Bea said.

Do you even know how many of those characteristics you share, Casildo?

"Want a kiss for luck?"

"No."

"I might need one."

"Answer's still no." Bea dropped her voice.

"Why are you whispering?" He leaned toward her.

"Because your mother's watching from the front bay windows.

"Al'ama! Thanks for the save."

Had he been serious? Since their kiss—kisses—in the café at the beginning of the week, even their almost kiss last night, the air between them had changed. He'd been more subtly affectionate, touching her occasionally, resting his shoulder against hers when she stirred something at the stove, watching her with a look in his eyes she couldn't define, but which gave her goose bumps. They'd each revealed more. She'd had dinner with her sisters to prevent her from sharing more.

Fat lot of good that did.

I went on a picnic today, snuggled into him until there wasn't a centimetre between us, then barely breathed hoping he'd do more than kiss my hair.

He hadn't spelled out his plans, but he'd admitted to a

side hustle. If textile design was his side hustle, he'd have his hands full.

Bea had confessed to being unavailable, but hadn't revealed the specifics.

So, attraction, but no future. They were clear on the rules.

"Let's make a move," he said.

Bea followed him the short distance to the front door. She'd worn the kind of outfit she'd wear for an informal work function. Wide, loose dark trousers, topped by a Made590 shirt, which her family had pooled funds to buy for her last birthday. She rubbed the soft voile between her fingers. A gorgeous shirt and the spurt of guilt spiked without warning, threatening to pierce her new-found pleasure at her independence.

I did not abandon them.

Cas unlocked the front door before bellowing, "Mum, Dad, it's me."

"That'll tell them." Bea followed him into the foyer, leaving the door ajar.

His mother emerged from a room off the hall, making it obvious she'd been watching for them through the front windows.

"I saw you arrive." Pleasure lit her face. "Welcome, Beatriz. I'm glad you could come." She embraced Casildo. "Habibi, are you well?"

"Thank you for the invitation, Mrs. Hariri." Bea glanced around the gracious foyer. From this brief exposure, the Hariris favoured a mix of Middle Eastern and Western décor. The lush wall hanging on the far wall made her fingers itch.

"You called me Farah at the wedding. Let's stick with that."

Bea's mother hadn't invited Casildo to use her first name. Part of that was her mother's old-fashioned manners, part that she thought Casildo was Hunter's friend, not hers.

"I'm good, Al'umu. Are we first?" Casildo asked.

Another car pulled into the driveway.

"Looks like Maha and Antonio have arrived." Farah stepped through the open door.

"You can touch it." Casildo appeared at her elbow. "I won't tell anyone." Then his gaze shifted toward the staircase. "Dad, you remember, Beatriz?"

His father reached the lobby. "Of course, I do. Welcome to our home, Beatriz. Casildo said you're missing Anna. We're missing Hunt. Crazy really. They've only been gone a week, but families are allowed to miss the people they love."

Another spurt of guilt pierced Bea. She wasn't missing her younger sisters. She did miss her parents, especially Mamá. "I had a message from Anna. Just the one word-heaven, but I guess that says it all," Bea replied.

"Mine said—and then some. They must have expected us to share." Cas's grin was wicked.

"Before the horde arrive, call me Raed." The older man's grin matched his son's.

"Are you calling Antonio a horde?" Casildo asked.

"Your mother and Maha can be a horde of avenging angels when the mood is on them."

Farah Hariri came first, followed by Maha and Antonio. Lots more hellos and kissing and hugging, and Antonio exchanged a quick look with Bea, which seemed to say *Brace yourself*.

"Hi, Antonio. How are you bearing up with Anna away?" Bea stood to one side of the hall.

"We're learning to cope. Have you heard anything?"

"Just that they're happy," she answered.

"Good, but that's not a surprise. Thanks for coming. Maha said Cas called you in as reinforcements. You're going to stage some kind of diversion if things get tricky. Can't wait to see the notoriously unflappable Beatriz Gomez staging a distraction."

"Tricky in what way?"

"They might ask me my intentions." He dragged a hand through his hair. "No one's asked me my intentions in two decades."

"What am I supposed to do?"

What has Casildo promised I'll do?

"Spill your drink, faint, take a phone call about a death in the family, declare undying devotion to Cas. Use your imagination. Hasn't Cas warned you?"

"Not that I'd be declaring undying devotion to him."

"That was an example," said Antonio.

"What are your intentions?"

"We haven't got further than deciding we like each other. It's not just us."

"Are you worried about the cross-cultural stuff?" Bea asked. Inter-cultural marriages could be tricky, especially when children were involved.

"I'm worried about my sons, about Maha's hopes and dreams. Neither of us are children. Hell, I won't see forty again, and I'm babbling."

"I'll spill my drink," Bea whispered. "What's the signal?"

"Hell, we haven't even worked out a signal." Antonio's frown cleared. "But I was joking. I hope I was joking."

"In families like ours, intentions are never a joke."

Turned out Antonio didn't need a signal. The first course passed without even vaguely skating near tricky territory.

"C'mon, Antonio," Casildo teased. "You must have some idea of where they went for their honeymoon."

"Anna just got all gooey-eyed when anyone asked her."

"Anna? Gooey-eyed? That's our warrior princess you're talking about." Casildo scoffed, resting his knee against hers under the table.

"Where do you think they've gone?" Farah asked, with a secret smile.

"I know that smile." Maha pointed at her mother. "Who blabbed, Hunt or Anna?"

"No one blabbed. I just have second sight," Farah said

demurely. "If you'll excuse me, I'll just get the next course."

"Sneaky." Casildo rose to help his mother with the dishes.

"No pumping your mother while you're in the kitchen," Raed called to their retreating backs, before turning back to Antonio. "I'm guessing you've known Anna a long time?"

"She joined the company more than a decade ago. She's incredible."

"We think she's incredible, but you probably know a different side of her," Raed continued.

Maha exchanged a look with her, and Bea guessed Maha already knew this story.

"My wife was diagnosed with cancer not long after Anna arrived. For a while there, I was AWOL. Anna didn't take over, but she marshalled the troops. She and a handful of others made sure I had a business to return to."

"We're happy for her and Hunter, happy she's part of our family."

In the lull created by Raed's words, Casildo pushed a trolley with plates and serving dishes into the room, and the next few minutes disappeared with plates being passed around and loaded.

"Maha said you have children," Farah picked up the conversation.

"Two. Boys," Antonio grinned. "Teenagers now, and I can't believe the time went so fast."

"In the blink of an eye." Raed looked from his son to his daughter to his wife. "I can't believe I'm a grandfather."

"Believe it, Farah said. "We've got them for the weekend."

Bea relaxed, kicking Casildo gently under the table to catch his eye, silently sending the message *You exaggerated. Your parents are pussycats.*

"So, Beatriz—"

Casildo grinned.

Farah passed a slice of black forest cake to Bea, and continued, "Did you meet Casildo through Anna?"

"Actually, we've probably known each other about five years. In our industry you tend to see the same faces again and again. Isn't that right, Casildo?"

"We've been stuck in enough hotel lobbies for me to learn she's the oldest of five daughters."

And that lifeline lasted through dessert, coffees and final farewells.

CHAPTER SEVEN

Cas followed Antonio's car out of his parents' drive, watched it turn right and promptly drive into what looked like the back entrance to the house. Cas smiled inwardly.

Way to go, sis.

"The granny flat?" Beatriz asked.

"The very one," he solemnly agreed.

"Do you think your mum and dad guess?"

"No. They're sure, and they're both happy and scared for Maha."

"My parents were like that with my two married sisters. Saw that their baby was in love and wondered if her fiancé loved her equally."

"In my family, it's whether his or her partner loves her as she deserves to be loved."

"The other night you said someone who can't bear to live without you."

"Pretty much the same thing. Everyone deserves someone in their life who thinks they're the most important person in the world."

Someone who chooses me, not my inheritance.

In Cas's experience, women and money didn't mix. Or rather, after a lifetime of blighted hopes, Cas was never sure why a woman was with him.

"I like Antonio," Cas admitted. "Like how he runs his business, how he treats his staff. All public-facing stuff. But, I don't know a lot about the man or his history. He's got two kids. That's only an issue if they resent his relationship with Maha. Mum and Dad would love more grandchildren."

"So, what's the problem?"

Cas didn't answer at first, navigating the car around the twists and turns leading to the secure carpark under Anna's building before parking in the allocated place. The engine died, and he didn't move.

"Maha's the best of us. I don't ever want her to be hurt. And that's craziness talking, because she's been hurt in the past and will be hurt in the future. That's life. But if she lets herself love Antonio, it will be with her whole heart and soul. She deserves to be given the same. No shadows lurking in corners."

"You love family, kids. Why aren't you married Casildo?"

"A misspent youth."

And the woman who claimed to be carrying my child lied to me.

He'd doubted the child was his. His relationship with Monique had been volatile. He'd made the mistake of thinking volatile equalled passionate, equalled monogamous. He'd taken precautions, but mistakes happened.

The dates worked.

Cas had been punch drunk, desperate to avoid a messy scandal that would shame his parents, and planning the wedding, when Maha and Hunt had locked Cas in a room and told him being honourable when the baby wasn't his was lunacy. Monique had been seeing at least one other person at the pertinent time. Social media didn't lie. The graphics were also explicit enough to identify some of Monique's companions.

Prenatal DNA testing confirmed Cas wasn't the father of Monique's child.

A flaming argument, with him largely silent, exposed the ugly truth. Monique had seen his parents' home and decided he was the better long-term breadwinner.

"What does a misspent youth mean?"

"Sometimes people are more interested in what my family has to offer than in me."

And what idiot just confessed that?

"Are you saying you've had girlfriends who assumed you'd inherit that"—she gestured over her shoulder in the direction they'd come from—"and that was what attracted them to you?"

"That's a blanket statement. But yeah, I've dated the odd woman or two who turned out to expect sparkly presents and exotic holidays." Or a trust fund for her and her unborn child.

"I'd laugh, except you sound so serious. Are you saying all those women whose heads turn when you pass are interested in your bank balance?"

"Forget it."

"You can't seriously believe you're only what your family has to offer?" She sounded dismayed.

"Once upon a time I did."

Saying the words made Monique past tense. And that was a relief and a new shock. Kissing Beatriz changed everything. There was no turning back after he'd tasted Beatriz. After her warmth had burned through him. Beatriz was the perfect antidote to Monique's double-dealing. The final stain from that time was the disappointment he'd seen in his father's eyes, but he was working on fixing that.

"Past tense is good. You're the attraction, Cas. You've got it all. Brains, body, and the emotional intelligence to see a woman as a person. I could list the number of women in our professional circle who'd love to date you. Dolly's completely genuine, and she'd adore to be seen on your arm."

"No disrespect to Dolly, but she must be twice my age."

"But genuine." She nudged him with her elbow.

"Why aren't you married, or hooked up or involved or something?" He circled a finger in the air.

"Dad had an industrial accident after I joined TBR. His recovery was slow." Her voice dropped lower. "To be honest, he's still not completely recovered."

Cas had the answer for why she'd disappeared from the scene for a while. And why she'd been more careful around people when she returned.

"I'm sorry. It hurts to discover your parents aren't invincible." He leaned across her to push open her door and caught a whiff of her delicious scent. Having her close helped to exorcise the sad memories that had joined them in the car. "Time to head upstairs. Want hot chocolate?"

"Your mother's dessert was so rich I couldn't even consider it."

"Tea and a debrief?"

Beatriz cocked her head to one side. "Okay."

What was she thinking?

Cas filled the kettle. "Black or more of the ginger?"

"Black's fine."

Once made, Cas carried it into the loungeroom. He took the armchair opposite the sofa. She nestled in her special corner. He'd like to nestle with her.

Stay right where you are, Cas.

She hadn't used first person when she'd said Cas was attractive, whereas his resistance got lower the more time he spent with her. Time to change the topic.

"What do you know about Antonio?"

"Why would I know anything?" She sipped her tea, but the furrow between her eyes told him she was considering how to answer.

"C'mon, girls talk." At her silent stare, he amended that. "Guys talk too, but it's not the same."

"You want to know if Antonio's personally honourable?"

"Yeah." His turn to stare into his cup.

"From everything Anna's said, the answer is yes. No ifs,

buts, maybes. No stray hand where it shouldn't be, no promise of a better desk, or office or promotion in return for favours."

"Has that happened to you?" Cas pushed himself up in the chair, suddenly alert.

"In the early days. Not so much now."

"Because you're old?

"That gave my self-esteem a boost."

"You're beautiful, Beatriz. You must know that."

"Old *and* beautiful. That's an improvement."

"*Older*. Do I need to talk to someone?"

"Not on my account." She studied him over her mug, then seemed to come to a decision. "I'm a fast learner. I changed companies. I swap stories with colleagues, especially new female employees, so none of us is caught in the wrong place at the wrong time. TBR's CEO is pretty good at sidelining the sleaze, but it means we have a faster staff turnover than some companies, and their recruitment practices need more work."

"Are you talking about Jackson Smithers?"

"He *is* a sleaze. He hasn't made any moves since his promotion." She hesitated.

"But?"

"He watches me, as if I'm a mouse who'll walk into the trap he's set." She shivered.

"Don't be alone with him."

"I don't plan to be. It's okay, Casildo. If he lays a finger on me, I'll scream. And I'm probably imagining things."

"Is that why you want your own business?" He scowled. "To control recruitment?"

"I'd like to choose my own clients, decide where to put the emphasis in a campaign. Choosing my own staff is a plus, but I imagine I'd be working on my own for a while."

"You'll get there."

"That's a better compliment." She toasted him with her empty mug. "But you were asking whether or not Antonio is honourable with women. I'd say yes."

"I'm being an idiot."

"A brotherly idiot. I don't think honour or decency are the barriers to Antonio and Maha having a relationship."

Cas forced himself to list the reasons why he and Beatriz shouldn't get down and dirty. Increasingly, they seemed irrelevant. They were consenting adults. If they decided to act on their attraction, it was no one's business but theirs.

* * *

Late Monday morning, Bea was typing up her notes from a client meeting when her boss knocked on her door.

"Got a moment?"

"Can I help with something?" Bea asked.

"That new idea we discussed. Something's come up." Martin took the seat in front of her desk.

Please let it be something real, something interesting that gets me out of this office and away from the barbarian for a few hours.

"A new client, keen to expand his printing business," Martin explained. "It's his first time considering an agency. He's run his own ads, got some loud signs on his business, but wants to know a bit more about how we can help him."

"Where is he?"

"Currently manning a booth at the Digital Arts Show. I said you'd drop over and see him this afternoon. It's at the Sydney Showground. Might be worth getting there early, so you can see who he's mixing with."

"It's a competitive field," she murmured. "Any instructions?"

"He figures he's got a few technological innovations to make him stand out and wants to parlay that into a brand known to be at the cutting edge." He stood to leave. "It's the kind of project that plays to your strengths, Beatriz. I'll leave it with you."

I have to tell Casildo.

I've got news.

She texted the second Martin left the room.

Snap. I've got news too. Wanna meet?
Zumba Cafe, bottom of George Street, thirty minutes.
See you there.

"This is a new one on me," Casildo said, gesturing to the café, when she arrived breathless thirty-five minutes later.

"Sorry, I'm late. It took me longer than expected to check a few things. I'll be catching a tram, so needed to come in this direction." She took his arm. "Let's find a seat."

"Is the tram the reason for your news?"

"My boss has delivered on his promise." She laughed.

"Congratulations."

"Who knew a simple meeting and a bit of a kissing in a public coffee house would trigger a series of different conversations with Martin."

"Only took him a week," grumbled Casildo. "*Bit* of kissing? I might have to work on my skills."

"You never asked what score I gave you?" she teased.

"That's because someone told me it was demeaning." He looked down his nose at her. "What do you want? I think we have to order at the counter."

"Just coffee, I'm too excited to eat."

Watching Casildo waiting to order, Bea reflected on his wide protective streak. She'd had to swallow her tears last night when he'd talked about what he wanted for Maha, what his hopes for love were.

Cas loved deeply, totally, endlessly. She wanted a man who'd love her like that, and she'd never said it aloud. Barely allowed herself to think it. And life held shadows and unexpected pitfalls and family. Yet a man like Casildo wouldn't crowd or try to control her thoughts or actions. He planted seeds. Anna understood the game Bea was in, and they chatted work occasionally, but on a superficial level. Casildo demanded she stretch boundaries and test new ideas.

"What's the job?" He sat down.

"Don't know yet. I'm meeting the client at the Digital Print Show to chat."

"I'm envious. The date popped up in my calendar. I've been mentally shifting projects to see if I can fit in a visit."

"I'll take photos for you."

"Is that all you've got? Digital Print Show?" He nodded to the waiter who brought their coffees.

"A bit more, but that's all I can share now."

"I can't get to the show this year, but I've got a consolation prize. A contact has offered me free tickets to the Lost Trades Fair in Bendigo, plus accommodation for a few nights. Someone dropped out at the last minute," he said.

"That's on my bucket list." She flopped back in her chair.

"I've been a few times. I always learn something new. Not just about textiles, although they've got a Saori, free-form, weaver there this year that I'd like to see. They've also got woodworkers. I've learned a bit about wood since Anna's brother-in-law is a carpenter."

"Anna said the sideboard in the lounge is one of his. Her own Niall Quinn design."

"He's generous with family and friends. You have to be careful not to admire a piece or you might find it on your doorstep. He offered to help Hunt out with refurbishing the childcare centre when he thought Hunt was short of labourers."

"I have a vague recollection of Anna mentioning some hiccup." Anna hadn't shared any details.

"It was a stuff-up with an order. The materials didn't arrive, so no work could be done on the childcare centre. Despite being in a major snit at Hunt at the time, Anna sent her brother-in-law to offer help."

"She just looks tough."

"No, Anna *is* Toledo steel tough, and I bless her daily for that." Casildo placed his hand on Bea's arm. "Do you think you can wrangle a day's leave at the end of this week?"

"What did you have in mind?" Bea held her breath, his light touch and the promise of a day with him sending her nerves skittering.

"I've got two tickets to the fair. Maha will swap her van for my car for the trip. It'll take a day to get there, a day to see the show, and a day back, but the drive's scenic in parts, and I can play you my full repertoire of jazz on the way. What do you think?"

"Are you inviting me?" she asked.

He swivelled his head from left to right. "I don't know anyone else here, Beatriz."

"Yes." Bea sighed. Not a single one of her past dates had suggested an outing so close to her soul. "It's a dream come true. What if I prefer country music?"

"Jazz on the way down, country on the way back." He liked negotiating as much as she did. "And I'm making a sacrifice with that offer."

"You're on. And I was teasing about the country music."

"Country music works in the country." He shrugged.

"You"—Bea pointed a finger—"are such a city boy. Are we staying with your contact?"

"No, it was a package deal at a local motel; a combined promo for the show and Bendigo's amenities."

"Tell me more about the accommodation." A holiday, a hotel and Casildo. "We don't want any more crossed wires about accommodation."

He pulled a folded piece of paper from his back pocket and handed her the printout of the information he'd been sent. "A two-bedroom unit. Small, but it's all there in the fine print. They even have pictures."

"Two bedrooms." Bea glanced at the page, then at him, stifling the fantasy that had flashed into her head. Only rom-coms included a scene with one bed. "It looks legit."

"When was the last time you took a holiday, Beatriz?"

"I can't remember."

"Your dreamy look says you recall it vividly."

"Anna talked me into a girls' weekend with her sister not long after I met her. Kate has a hideaway a few hours outside Sydney."

"Why wasn't I told that?"

"Because it's her bolthole. Probably her and Liam and Lily's bolthole these days. When we visited, Kate was living full-time in the cottage."

"I've only met Kate a few times, but she strikes me as a city girl."

"She was hiding from some weird boyfriend who was hassling her."

"Anna has more reasons than I thought to hate entitled men. Did Anna find her the bolthole?"

"Anna said she bought her apartment and Kate bought the cottage with a legacy from their maternal grandmother."

"I loved my maternal grandmother. Still miss her."

"You said the granny flat was built for her. What was the name you called her?"

"Jaddatee. I think I told you Grandpa died. Mum refused to leave Jaddatee behind. They delayed until Mum could convince Jaddatee to come."

"What's her actual name?"

"Wahida," he crooned. Just saying her name made Casildo smile. "Do you know your grandparents?"

"For a long time it was letters and phone calls, then video calls. They live with family on the maternal and paternal sides. It's the grandkids who handle the tech hook-ups these days. Mamá really missed her mum, especially when my sisters were little."

"You picked up the slack. So, Beatriz Gomez, are you coming with me?"

"Try and stop me. I'm finding rebellion easier the more I practise."

CHAPTER EIGHT

Beatriz smiled at the crowd surging through the huge hall housing the Digital Print Show. The client she'd just farewelled was already mixing it with some of the bigger guys, keen to expand his reach and open to new ideas.

"Thank you, Casildo," she whispered in her head, then spent a few seconds imagining other ways she might thank him, all of which involved climbing onto his lap and seeing where a bit of bodily heat took them.

The last ten days of sharing an apartment had been a revelation. He was incredibly easy to live with. He pulled his weight on chores, was considerate in small ways and worked punishing hours if you added up what he did in his office with whatever he did in that boxy little room down the hall. She hadn't been brave enough to invite herself in there yet.

"Hey. Have you got a moment?"

Bea turned toward the voice. Ordinary-looking guy, dark colouring, about Casildo's age, sporting a very obvious wedding ring. "Can I help you?"

"I don't know that you can." He smiled, a rueful quirk of the lips that set her completely at ease. A boy-next-door smile. "But I overheard a bit of what you were saying. "You're in advertising."

"I work for an advertising company."

"That's a trick answer, but I'm a complete ignoramus in that area."

"Is this your stall?" She gestured to the booth bearing the same name as his T-shirt. It sported a huge banner promoting computerised printing. The trade fair was filled with booths, small and large, and her client was the resident of a booth nearby—not a big project, but an interesting one.

"The family business." He nodded.

"Computerised printing is top of the pops these days. I see you handle textiles and fabric."

"We do." Another rueful smile. He jutted his chin in the direction of her jacket. "You prefer older style fabrics. And natural dyes."

"You recognise the competition." She laughed.

"I dreamed of being a purist."

"Are you looking to promote your business? Is that why you approached me?"

"Do you know Casildo Hariri?"

"Different company, but I know him." She smiled. "Why?"

"Maybe you could say hello. That sounds lame."

"Why do you need a go-between?"

"We've been out of touch in recent years."

"Occupational hazard." She glanced meaningfully at his banner.

"Cas is a purist, but that's not why we've lost touch. Have you got time for a drink?"

She glanced at her watch. "I went off the clock a few minutes ago, so as long as you're not trying to ferret trade secrets out of me or pump me about your neighbour's plans"—she pointed a thumb over her shoulder—"we should be good."

"I'm a stranger. I could be trying to pump you. Why agree?"

She grinned. "You said the magic word. Casildo. For him, you get a friendly chat in a public place. And, my lungs are in perfect working order if I made the wrong call."

* * *

Can you meet me in the bar at the Empire Hotel in Paddington?
I've got a surprise for you.

Casildo stared at Beatriz's text. An invitation to an after-work drink with his very attractive flatmate was a surprise because when they'd parted earlier, the plan was dinner at the apartment.

He glanced at his watch.

I can be there in fifteen.

When Cas strolled through the door, he didn't spot them immediately, had almost finished circling the downstairs bar, when he caught sight of Beatriz's tiger jacket. They were sitting at a corner table, half-hidden by another group. The man spotted Cas before Beatriz did, rising to his feet.

"Mo. This is a surprise." Cas wrapped his college friend in a one-armed hug.

"A good one, I hope." Mo gave his slow, serious smile, the one that reached his eyes.

"Very. How are you?" Cas had understood Mo's decision to withdraw from their fledgling business partnership three years ago. When Mo fell in love with Evie, Mo's father had offered his only son the assistant manager's role in their fabric printing business. *"This is your future now, son."*

"Better than I've been in a while."

Cas turned to Beatriz. "I like your idea of a surprise."

"Good." She smiled and rose to her feet. "Now, you're here, I'll make a move." She walked toward him, then patted his chest.

Cas inhaled the citrusy scent he'd come to associate only with her—fresh and tart. Or out of the ordinary and honest.

"It's my turn to cook dinner." She turned to Mo. "I'll be in touch."

"Can I get you a drink?" Mo asked when they were

alone.

"Bitters and soda with fresh lemon if they've got it."

Mo returned to the table with the drink and raised his. "Here's to chance meetings."

"To chance meetings," Cas agreed. Finding Beatriz in Anna's apartment had been a chance meeting.

"I like your new girlfriend."

"Beatriz isn't my girlfriend." Denial was automatic, but the idea held increasing appeal.

"It's just her turn to cook dinner. Right!" Mo's right eyebrow shot up.

"Short-term flatmates. And you didn't hear that."

"Hear what?"

"Strictly platonic."

"Coming from anyone else, I'd say bullshit. You, I believe. Heard you and Monique broke up. Monique shared your perfidy—I love that word, although I had to look it up—with the world. She called you deceitful and untrustworthy. It'd be funny if it wasn't so outrageously wrong."

"It was messy." Messy was an understatement that still gave Cas the occasional sleepless night.

"Then I can say what I think. Monique was poisonous. You must know that."

Cas didn't know how much Mo knew. Cas had withdrawn for a while, needing time to get his head around what had happened. "My family's rumoured wealth still turns a lot of women on. And to be fair to her, I was distracted, not paying enough attention to her."

"Crap. You and she were never going to last. She knew it and tried to blackmail you into marriage."

"I should have broken it off with her sooner."

"I don't think that would have made a blind bit of difference once she'd made up her mind. She left town when word got around about what she tried to do." Mo held his gaze.

"Great. The world knows I'm an idiot. I had casual sex

with a woman. I didn't take sufficient precautions against pregnancy, and I didn't break it off sooner because I enjoyed the convenient sex." Those were the failures that had upset his dad.

"You might have started out thinking with your dick, but ultimately you were a victim. You would have accepted full responsibility for Monique, and for a child who wasn't yours. She'd have bled you dry." Mo's voice was matter-of-fact. "I outed her in our old circle."

"Al'ama. Why?" Cas absorbed the shock. Monique's bad-mouthing of him had died away quickly. At the time, he'd wanted to forget everything.

"Bea's nice."

"How does that connect to anything?" Cas growled.

"Told me I was being an idiot not approaching you."

"Do you need something? Is Evie okay?"

"I've missed you." Mo grimaced. "And that's the why. You're a genuinely good guy. Outing Monique was all I could do for you. I've barely had time to breathe in the last few years."

"You're good now? Evie's good?"

"Losing Alice knocked us both for six. We want—wanted—children. Evie just got pregnant sooner than anticipated. I nearly lost them both. You knew that. The miscarriage and then the news Evie couldn't have children landed us in a dark place." Mo sipped orange juice. No additives, Mo was teetotal. "Maha held Evie while she screamed and threw things at the wall. Held me too. Truth be told."

"She never told me."

"No surprises there. Maha let slip one day what Monique had done. I don't know if she intended me to say something or hoped I would. I guess she worried no one would believe her. But, there was Monique treating an unborn child like a meal ticket, when I would have cut off my right arm to save Evie and my baby."

"Maha didn't tell me that either."

"The secrets your sister knows." Mo shook his head, his grin devilish.

"How's Evie?"

"Wonderful. We've applied to a foster agency. Maha is our referee." Mo took another pull on his drink. "How'd your mum and dad take the news about Monique?"

"They were gracious, welcoming—" His father's expression of regret was etched into Cas's soul.

"But disappointed?"

"Yeah."

"That's what gets you with dads like ours. That dog-sad look of disappointment as if you'd stolen their last bone before you abandoned them on a rocky archipelago. I reckon they practise in a mirror, and I reckon your parents have had a lot fewer regrets about their children than the average."

Cas let that pass. Maha, Zahra, and Hunt were children to be proud of.

"I heard your dad had to sell the family flagship building." Mo glanced sideways at him. "Then I heard Hunter had bought it and decided there might be a public and private version of that story as well."

"You're right. The financial markets have been unreliable, the pandemic shifted some tenancy and occupancy patterns, and Dad faced a hostile takeover." He paused, swallowed another mouthful of his drink. "From Nick Richardson."

"Hunter's dad?"

"Yep," Cas said, knowing Mo wouldn't share the news.

"Hell, are you and Hunter okay? Is your dad okay?"

"Hunt and I are good. Dad's okay about the sale, but it changed something in him. I'm not sure what." He could trace the change back to Monique's arrival in his parents' home. And that was a conversation he hadn't had with Hunter yet. "I moved back in for a while." That wasn't a lie, but it provided cover for his silence over ... far too long.

"Welcome to the club." Mo shrugged. "Fathers have a

way of bringing us to heel."

Cas wanted to dispute that, because he'd resurrected his textile design business dream and was finetuning the details. Operating a successful business venture might remove the disappointment from his father's eyes. Cas was sweating on it.

"I might finally have shifted some attitudes in my family." Mo nursed his drink.

"A machismo-culture bypass? Is that even a thing?"

"My baby sister, Suzy, already thinks she can replace me."

Cas laughed. "She was always fearless."

"I didn't thank you enough at the time for just accepting that I had to pull the plug on us. You were entitled to go ballistic. I made promises to you."

"Who was it who said, 'A smart man changes his mind when circumstances change'? You had no choice, Mo."

"For a long time, it looked like Evie and I had no choices. But I wouldn't swap her for anyone."

Cas nudged him. "Did you really spread gossip about Monique?"

For Cas, Monique remained a bad dream. She was no longer in his life. The lasting damage was his sense that he'd failed to live up to his father's expectations.

"Evie was the demon. She knew who to talk to."

"Thanks."

"She did it as much for Maha as you. Your sister still calls and drops in. Evie adores her."

"Maha has that effect on people."

Mo studied his drink. "I let you down, Cas."

"No, you didn't." Cas had had plenty of time to think about this. "You made the same choice I would have made in your situation."

"You don't think it was the final effect of that drip-feed we'd had since birth—'*You need a steady job and a steady income if you want to take a wife. You must have something to offer a woman.*'"

"I can hear my dad and your dad now."

"I love Evie. I did and do want to build a life with her. I did feel the pressure to make a steady income. I don't regret my decision. I'm sorry you were collateral damage."

"No biggie." Cas had understood Mo's decision and persisted with his own side of the partnership dream.

Cas had a fresh portfolio of designs. Ones he hadn't shown to any of the businesses he'd worked with in the past. New designs to launch his business. Design was something he could do, given everything else was on hold. Although, with his father saying he'd have the money within weeks, Cas had restarted a few conversations. And he was feeling both excited and hopeful.

Beatriz makes me feel hopeful.

"About Beatriz. Different companies, but we tend to bump into each other at functions. We've been friendly competitors for at least five years."

"And flatmates for … ?" Mo wasn't pushing.

"This is week two. We're both bunking down in Anna's flat while she and Hunt are on their honeymoon. That doesn't explain why the capable Ms. Gomez met you at the Digital Print Show to discuss new opportunities."

"She didn't come to meet me. Husic Fabric Printing has a booth at the show. We've done well in recent years with digital printing. Got a cushion under the business. That's really why Dad wanted me to become more involved. I understood tech better than him. Suzy's totally obsessed."

"Could she take over?"

"In a heartbeat." Mo shrugged. "Recently, I've been mulling over some different ideas, but looking to fly below the radar until I'm a little clearer about what I can do. I was minding my own business, had left my stall, when I overheard Ms. Gomez talking to another stallholder. I'm guessing he's the new opportunity. He seemed smitten."

"She's exceptional at her job."

"I believe you. When she finished with him, I door-stopped her. You've stopped taking commissions?" Mo jutted his chin, his words halfway between a question and a statement.

"You've been following me?"

"I've got an interest."

"It's been a bad year," Cas admitted. Mo had shared Cas's dream through college and for years afterward, so deserved the truth from him. "I'm mulling my next steps too."

"That's how your name came up," Mo said.

"Not sure I understand."

"I was talking to Ms. Gomez, who said to call her Bea, about the old days and old dreams."

"She's good at her job if she got you to open up."

"You already said she's exceptional."

"Tell her boss."

"Okay. But let's finish this conversation. I mentioned your name. She said she knew you, offered to call you. I don't know what you're thinking. Bea didn't offer any insights." Mo waved his glass in the air. "Different companies and all that."

"All that." Cas grinned.

"I might have some ideas. Husic's is considering branching out."

"I'm open to ideas." A weight eased inside Cas. Mo had been the perfect yin to his yang when they'd worked together. The world had turned, Mo had new priorities, but anything he had to say would be valuable.

"I need to go now. Evie's expecting me." Mo placed a hand on his sleeve. "I'll be in touch. And Evie would love to see you. Come to dinner."

"I'd love to catch up with her."

"Bring Bea."

Beatriz Gomez—my flatmate, not my girlfriend, the star of my fantasies, perceptive enough to get Mo to talk to me, sensitive enough to leave us alone.

CHAPTER NINE

Cas found Beatriz in the kitchen still in her work outfit.

"I went back to the office," she said apologetically. "I'll get changed, then start dinner."

"I'll call for a pizza. Let's take the night off."

"Thank you. Now, I've met your friend Mo, who's Evie?"

Beatriz yawned, stretching her arms above her head and doing a little shimmy at the same time. He had to bite his tongue not to say "Do it again."

"Didn't you ask?"

"Mo and I don't have a professional or personal relationship. Remember. I was there for the other bloke— my reward for being so sweet about Jackson Smithers."

Cas followed her into the living room, pressing buttons on his phone. "Pizza ordered. Twenty to thirty minutes. They're busy. I know your boss Martin. He did not say *sweet.*"

"It was in his tone. His words were '*Thank you for your ongoing support of Jackson. He's learned a lot from you.*'" She shucked her jacket, then sank onto the sofa and heeled off her boots.

"They last longer if you undo them and slip them off."

"Thank you, Papá."

"So, it's rebellion, not laziness driving your behaviour."

"Lovely word 'rebellion.' I've never rebelled against a blessed thing. See, I couldn't even manage a damn then." She sighed loudly.

"And from what you said earlier, I bet you didn't knee Martin in the balls because he worked out too late that you're the brains behind Jackson's ideas."

She giggled, and his cock stirred.

"I even kept to myself that Jackson wouldn't learn another blessed thing from me as long he lived. Back to Mo. He approached me as I was leaving the show. He overheard parts of my conversation."

"Old habits die hard. He was checking out the competition. That's what I'd do."

Since moving in with Beatriz, Cas was spending more time in the boxy spare room on his designs than his business plans.

"Checking out fabrics and dyes and new ideas. It becomes an addiction."

Designing for Beatriz was becoming an addiction. His designs were all pastels, because someone with Beatriz's energy needed a soothing place to sleep—and curves because Beatriz was his inspiration, and he wasn't sure these designs should be made public. He bent to pick up her boots and set them on the floor at the end of the sofa.

"What were your majors at college?"

"Business, marketing, art."

"Tell me about the art."

"Why don't you go and get changed?"

"Into something more comfortable?" She giggled. "They say that in old movies. It's a euphemism." She was adorable when she giggled.

"Is it now?" He'd play the game to the end.

"You slip into something comfortable as a prelude for slipping into nothing at all, and then you slip into bed."

"Are we going to bed?" *Say yes.*

"*You* are going to bed. *I* am going to bed. But in the time between now and then, we can share a pizza, then a hot chocolate and apparently *not* talk about your art major."

"Mo and I planned to start a business together. But he told you that. It's why you invited me along, then quietly disappeared."

"Tell me your side."

He removed her jacket from the back of the sofa and flopped down beside her, unable to resist rubbing the lapel between a finger and thumb.

"Mo has the expertise in printing. My contribution was the design. We're both pretty passionate about fabrics, but he has the deeper knowledge of what fabrics can take what colours and dyes. We had a rudimentary business plan. We were both working day jobs and doing this on the side."

"Any success?"

"Does that matter?"

"I imagine it mattered to you and Mo."

"We had some success. Did some bespoke designs for a few big brands, were nurturing contacts, gaining confidence and hoarding our coins."

I was hoarding my coins.

"Remind me again who Evie is?"

"You've worked out who Evie is." He set her jacket aside.

"Tell me anyway."

"Evie is Mo's wife. They've been married about three years now. She got pregnant sooner than expected."

"And Husic senior convinced his son that his future lay with digital printing, synthetic dyes and mostly synthetic fabrics."

"Evie had a miscarriage. Nearly died. The prognosis was no babies. Ever. So yeah, it was a sensible business decision, but the work helped him stay sane."

"They must have been devastated." She threaded her fingers through his, her instant sympathy comforting him as much as her touch.

"Yeah. They've signed up to be foster parents. They'll be good."

"Mo told me about Monique."

Cas absorbed the confession, because Beatriz was admitting she knew another one of his secrets. Time for him to admit he trusted Beatriz with all his secrets. She was the first woman to slip past his defences in … ever.

"My fault," she rushed on, releasing her hold on him, "if that's the right term. I couldn't imagine you walking away from a friendship because he joined his father's business. I asked why you'd lost touch. I wanted to know in case he'd done a number on you and organising a meet-up between you would be a monumental mistake. Mo said you had a girlfriend who'd done a number on you, and you'd gone off-air for a while."

"That's a thin outline," Cas said. And Mo had left it to Cas to fill in the details for Beatriz, if he chose to. "Mo told me he'd outed Monique."

"Not sure I follow."

"Mo and Evie lost a much-hoped-for baby. Monique told me she was carrying my child."

"I'm guessing that was a lie." She jabbed him in the chest. "What's with the surprised expression? You'd never have walked away from a child."

Beatriz wasn't outraged or suspicious. More importantly, she wasn't disappointed in him for the simple reason she didn't believe he'd abandon a woman carrying his child. A tension Cas had been holding for what seemed like forever drained out of him.

"She banked on that. And I mean banked."

"So, Mo blew her cover. Then what?"

"Actually, Maha and Hunt worked it out. Locked me in a room until I agreed to a DNA test. I wasn't the father. Mo and Evie were raw from losing their baby and were disgusted at Monique's manipulation of an unborn child."

"I'm with them." She fiddled with the buttons on her waistcoat. "Are you over Monique?"

"I've accepted I was an idiot. But it hurt Mum and Dad. I hate that I dragged my family into that mess." Shame lingered, that he'd been so gullible.

Telling Beatriz eased some of the shame. Warmth swirled through him, a by-product of the trust and sheer intimacy of their conversation.

"I don't need to know the details. Mo also told me, he didn't get rid of the old machinery. That the wheel has turned in the marketplace. He's being approached by customers, by strangers. Even with his big glossy signs saying *computer printed* and *artificial dyes*. The interest in sustainable and reusable is growing."

"I read the trade journals, Beatriz. Follow the blogs. Sustainable is increasingly important across all industries. We both work for companies that promote sustainable practices to give them an edge."

"Of course we do. Did you hear the first part of what I said?"

"Something about the old machinery." Cas turned the idea over in his head.

"So your friend Mo Husic is thinking about getting back into the game. He wants a different location, a different brand, a different product range to separate it from their current business."

"He didn't mention that." A tickle of excitement ran down Cas's spine. Mo had mentioned ideas, said they've got a cushion under the business. A cushion was nothing to sneeze at. It gave you options.

"I gather he's in the very early stages and doesn't want to let you down a second time if he can't deliver. He said Evie wouldn't let his dream die. Evie insisted he keep the machinery, keep working on natural dyes. She surprised him with a new workshop in their yard. They're toying with the brand name Sunshine Superman or Save the Planet and Still Make Profits."

"You managed that with a straight face. Mo always was crap at business names. What would you call it?"

"Mo isn't one of my clients. So, are you going to lose touch again?"

"He said he'd call. I wish him all the luck in the world, but I'm not sure how it affects me." But it might shoot his plans forward faster than he'd dare hope. Mo was still perfect for the printing. And now Cas was at the pointy end of starting a business, he was beginning to appreciate the skills he lacked.

"What did you say your plans are?"

"They're not concrete." Cas had also realised Beatriz had all the business skills he lacked.

"And there's the issue of jinxing them if you speak them aloud. Uh-huh."

"Are you mocking my caution?"

"At the risk of pissing you off, and there's that spark of rebellion growing stronger—your fault because you encourage me—I went back and checked some business registers. Anna and Hunter's first meeting was one of those bizarre acts of fate. You brought him to a work function. They hit it off, until she discovered Hunter was the evil developer who'd swooped without warning and bought the building where she hoped to house her childcare centre. He cancelled her lease the day it was due to be signed."

"Incredible piece of luck taking Hunter that night." Cas had made enough confessions for one day.

"A records search shows the previous owner of the building was Raed Hariri. Is that the Raed Hariri I had dinner with last Sunday?"

"You did a records search." *Well, damn.*

"Due diligence it's called in my job." She smiled.

The sheer mischief in her expression landed low in his body, making him desperate to get his hands on her.

"You can tell me to mind my own business."

She paused, giving him plenty of time to say just that, but Cas wanted to tell her, to get her professional as well as her personal take on his ideas.

"Do your not-yet-concrete plans also have something to

do with Nick Richardson, Hunter's father?"

"He donated the sperm. He's not Hunter's father in any way that counts."

"That's telling me."

"Did you find anything else?" He tugged at his tie with one hand and pulled the coffee table into a reachable position. "I'm getting comfortable because you clearly have more to say." He lifted his feet.

She pressed a hand to his thigh. "Pizza's going to be served there soon."

"Pizza's designed to withstand football boots, jock straps and sweaty underarms."

"Not my pizza."

His phone pinged at that moment.

"Saved by the bell." She smiled smugly. "I'll get the cutlery."

"I'm eating from the box tonight."

"True confessions need cardboard? And you're a fabric guru."

"I'm a man of many parts." He returned with the pizza and set it on the table between them.

"I'm starving." She lifted a piece dripping with melted cheese to her mouth, took a bite and closed her eyes. "Yum."

Cas took a slice and bit in.

"Hunter outmanoeuvred Nick Richardson to buy your father's building. What's Nick's gripe with your family?"

Apparently, Cas hadn't made all the confessions he was going to make tonight.

"Nick hates us because Hunt loves us. Nick tried to bankrupt my father to hurt Hunter. He wanted to bring Hunter to heel." Cas had learned, from Hunter's experiences, from Mo, and from Monique's demand for a pre-nup with claims on Cas's father's business before trotting him up the aisle, that taking his medicine in one gulp resulted in the least long-term pain.

"Bring Hunter to heel how?" She selected a second slice

of pizza. "Four slices for me, six for you. We agree now."

"Or what?" He loved how she negotiated sharing. He figured it was being one of five sisters.

"I demand half."

"Deal. Nick is every bogeyman you've ever met come to life, an emotional vampire. He wanted to destroy Hunt and take over his business." Bitterness burnt Casildo's throat. Nick had got too close.

"Anna didn't tell me any of this."

"She's the best thing that ever happened to Hunt."

"You believe that, yet you've been at his side since childhood," she said, leaning into him. "Hunter would hate you to feel beholden to him."

"Beholden's the wrong word when it's family. You know that. Hunter is family. Dad and I tried to deflect Nick's attack before we called Hunter. A truckload of cash was needed."

She cocked her head to one side and studied him with the solemnity of a judge about to sentence. "You gave him your savings."

"You guessed."

"I put two and two together. You earn a decent wage, you don't have a profligate lifestyle, but you have a secret passion you've been working at for years."

"I was the logical child to help."

He'd been the only child with fast access to savings. Hunter's hands were full with his own company, Maha had tipped all her funds and energy into paying off her share of the childcare centre she ran with a friend, and Zahra was an intern at a busy public hospital juggling work and motherhood. Cas still battled private demons that he hadn't been able to save his father.

"It wasn't enough. Despite Dad and my reservations, Hunt would have been gutted if we'd lost the building without asking for his help." And maybe Cas needed to think about that flashbulb moment.

"What's the plan?"

Cas didn't pretend not to understand her question. It was a relief to let go of his fears of jinxing his plans, to accept that doubt was the unwanted shadow for anyone working in the creative industries. His dreams were safe with Beatriz. He liked the weight of her leaning against him.

"It was a temporary loan. The idea is that Dad rearranges his portfolio." He snorted. "I learned about that from my studies. "Then he buys Hunter out and gives me back my nest egg."

"Can he do that?"

"He's done it. Barring final legal hiccups, the money will be in my bank account before Anna and Hunt re-enter the country. Not that either of us are counting days."

"How do you feel about it?"

"I have to do this, Beatriz. I need to prove to my dad and myself I can."

"Why your dad?"

"Mo and I talked about that. Fathers cast long shadows. You always want to please them. Or at least not disappoint them."

"I watched your dad last Saturday night. He loves you and Maha, and"—she seemed to search for a word—"he was so happy being with you. Hard to improve on that. I'd say he's proud now."

"We're a business family. I'm the only child without a business." He knew his father loved him. He wasn't so sure he was proud of him. "I haven't made promises to anyone, but I'm making connections, appointments."

And you make me feel positive.

Another flashbulb moment he wasn't prepared for.

"And your worry about jinxing it is for those suppliers and other small businesses." She lifted his arm and draped it around her shoulders, snuggling against his side. "I knew there was a reason I liked you."

"Just the one?"

"Maybe more than one. You'll make it work."

"What?" he joked, because she had faith in him. "After

I work out what I'm looking for in a property."

"You know what you're looking for, but you could always ask your dad or Hunter for advice."

"They might jinx it."

"You're a dope."

Later when they stood side by side in the kitchen, him washing and her drying their beer glasses and cutlery, she hip-bumped him. "You've gone strangely silent."

"Bad habit. I often live in my head."

She deserves to know all my bad habits. Maybe that's the way to keep it in my pants? I can list my flaws.

"Dreaming is positive. If you can't imagine a different future, you'll never achieve it." She sounded sombre.

"Do you dream, Beatriz?"

"All the time." She turned and rested her hips against the bench. "Will you show me some of your designs, please?"

He closed his eyes. "Yes."

"Now?"

"Let's make some hot chocolate first." He was babbling.

"You only drink hot chocolate to distract me."

"Does it work?" *Tell her a fault.* "The study's a bit messy."

She grinned. "Remember our pact? You can say no."

"Hot chocolate for two in the study."

"I'll make the hot chocolate." She patted his chest. "Give you time to hide anything you don't want me to see."

He was standing at his desk when she arrived with the two mugs.

"We need two chairs, Casildo."

"I'll get one."

He returned with an upright chair. Of necessity, they sat close together. Her thigh rested against his, her knee accidentally bumped his, her shoulder touched his, and he was ready to go up in flames. Wanting her and not acting on it left him permanently turned on.

"Can you start with some of your early ones, to give me

a sense of history?"

Her question settled him, giving him a place to start. He pulled a folder from the desk drawer. "These were the first we sold." He spread a half dozen drawings across the table.

She tucked her hands under the desk.

"You can touch them, Beatriz."

"They're beautiful. Did you study Arabic design, Saudi design? There's a hint of it."

She spent her days around designers. It wasn't her area of expertise, but Beatriz would have paid attention to the work and asked questions because that was how she operated. Understanding the layers that combined to send a message. Plus her clothes spoke to an interest in fabric and textile design as much as clothes design.

"At Jaddatee's knee. Only two women have held art exhibitions in Saudi Arabia. Jaddatee went to Safeya Binzagr's in 1968. She admired her enormously. Jaddatee could weave. Mum kept every piece she could. When Safeya opened the Darat Safeya Binzagr in 2000, Jaddatee had some friends send her photos. They included traditional artefacts, textiles, and costumes. Safeya Binzagr recently released a book. Maha bought it for me."

"That's a lovely story." She traced a delicate finger over one of the designs. It would suit her, but as what—a sofa cover, cushions, sheets? "And I envy your relationship with Maha."

"Why? You're close to your sisters, apart from the snafu that landed you here." He faced her.

"I love my sisters to bits, but I was born in Chile, then we moved to Australia. After a few years, sisters two and three were born, then after another big gap, sisters four and five. Two sets of two. Each pair is inseparable."

"Why the second big gap?"

"Mamá nearly died giving birth to Daniela."

"That's when you took over a lot of the child minding."

She nodded, dragged in a deep breath. "This isn't about me." She squeezed his knee, and the tingle shot straight through him, all cells on instant alert.

Pay attention, Cas.

"Umm." He took a sip of the chocolate, pretending his groan was in response to Hunt's idea of a liquid chocolate bar, rather than to the delicious Beatriz Gomez leaning into him, her hand still on his thigh while she questioned him. He'd confess about drawing his first design with a permanent Texta on his jaddatee's best white tablecloth soon. Or kiss her.

Something had to give.

"Have you got any recent designs?"

"Yes."

Tell her a flaw. Dilute the tension. I sometimes become obsessed and work all night. What woman wants to buy into that?

"Beatriz?"

She turned to face him, her beautiful eyes twinkling. "I'd rather kiss you. You can say no. Although, I was angling for that when I almost sat in your lap."

"'Come up and see my etchings'?" he managed a hoarse whisper.

"I asked, I'm genuinely interested and more than impressed."

"Are you talking about my designs or my kisses?"

"I haven't shared enough kisses with you to make a judgement."

"Let's see if we can do better. Just kisses though. We agreed this is a bad idea."

"Speak for yourself." She straddled his lap.

"I sometimes get obsessed and work all night."

"Is that a warning about your kisses?"

He didn't have time for a fling. She was driving him insane. No, his insistence that they not go beyond increasingly heated kisses was driving him insane.

"I'm only talking temporary." She linked both hands behind his neck.

Okay. I can make time. Except.

"You're not a casual-affair anything, Beatriz."

The truth was he didn't want to do casual with Beatriz. He'd been casual with Monique. She'd known it and tried to manipulate him. Beatriz was offering with no strings attached, when they were already woven together as tightly as fine tweed.

"I might be." She nibbled his ear. Beatriz Gomez was nuzzling his throat and nibbling on him.

He swallowed. "Right. In what universe?"

"This one. The universe in this apartment. No one knows we're here."

"Have you forgotten Hunt and Anna?"

"They don't know yet, and they won't blab it to the world." She rolled her eyes and tangled her fingers in his hair.

"Why?" Cas asked while he was still marginally in control.

"Jeez. Do you need a reason?" She pointed from herself to him.

I waited.

"I've got the hots for you. And I think you fancy me."

"Fancy has to be the most imprecise, useless, inaccurate word on the planet," he muttered. Cas was deeply attracted to Beatriz, but his plans were set.

Except I want more, but I don't ever want to hurt you.

"You're gorgeous. I want to touch you. Doesn't mean we should."

Although I might go crazy if I don't.

"Are we back to practising saying no?" She climbed off his lap, but tormented him by standing between his thighs.

His fault she'd withdrawn. His fight with himself over the right thing to do left them both aroused. His fingers itched to drag her straight back onto his lap.

"I am. I don't want to hurt you."

"Consenting adults here, Casildo. No harm, no foul."

"I'm about to risk every cent I have and throw in my job to follow a dream."

"You're doing this completely on your own?"

"Yes." His jaw clenched.

She touched it, her fingers soothing.

"I'm the odd man out in my business-oriented family. I need to make a success of it without family help to prove I can." Cas wanted to see his father's eyes light up with pride.

"I can see you do, and I'll be barracking for you as loudly as anyone. But, Casildo, you help your family." Her fingers made their way from his jaw to his ear. She gave a gentle tug, and his brain turned to mush. "They might want to help you, not because you can't do it alone but because they want to share your joy."

"I'm letting you know this can't go anywhere."

"Already dealt with that point. You're helping me feel better after a crap day."

"I snore."

She giggled.

"Hunt said I did. Once." Cas groaned, then pulled her back onto his lap before cupping her breast and nuzzling her throat, absorbing her.

"Uh-huh. Haven't heard you myself, and I like to make my own judgements." She gently nipped at his earlobe. "Hard to know what's the biggest deal breaker, snoring, working all night or being my best friend's husband's blood brother, who'll worry I'm taking advantage of you."

"Anna's more likely to worry I'm taking advantage of you." He moved until their lips almost met.

"They should be able to talk some sense into each other."

"You are making me feel better."

"I feel pretty good myself," she whispered.

Cas let her breathy gasp reverberate through him. Seconds, he waited seconds, savouring the sensation of breathing in time with her, feeding the lick of arousal into a flame, before he closed the gap. He caught her lower lip between his teeth, nibbling, then swallowing her moan of pleasure. Her scent surrounded him, pure Beatriz, and he wanted to shout his gratitude that she was here with him—

a woman he liked as much as he lusted after.

She pressed closer, open-mouthed, demanding entry. Pliant in his arms, a sweet armful of woman. Textures, she was a mass of textures—silky hair, satin-soft skin, the polished texture of her silk waistcoat—and his hands raced everywhere, wanting to imprint the sensations on his mind. Then, he lost himself in the kiss. Kisses, one leading to the next, straining to be closer. Better than in the café, better than their gentle exchange at the picnic. No one was watching, so they were free to run riot. Her hand slid under his shirt, her fingers trailed across his midriff, walked toward his nipple, and he sucked in a breath.

"We're not actually going anywhere tonight, Beatriz." He drew back, resting his forehead on hers. His breathing was ragged, his restraint shredded, but this was Beatriz. He was holding on tight to decency, or fairness or something. He didn't want Beatriz regretting this in the morning, regretting him.

"Damn you."

"We're making out."

"You do that when you're a kid in the back of your parents' car."

"Substitute Anna's flat for parents' car."

"You'd better lock your door." She wound her fingers through his hair and tugged. Hard.

Already aroused, the vibrations left his cock aching. *What did you say?*

"Pardon?" He stared at her.

"I've nearly walked through the last few nights."

"What were you wearing?" Stupid question when he'd just torture himself with images and fantasies of her later. Beatriz had left him more familiar with his right hand than he'd been in months.

"Sometimes, I'm naked." She breathed.

"Textures." He swallowed a moan. "I fantasise about the taste and feel of your skin."

"Me too," she confessed. "That's why I toy with the idea

of layers. A voile dressing gown then a sheer silk shoestring-strapped negligee before you find skin."

"I like the way you think," he groaned. "We'll take it slowly."

"We started with four weeks and the clock's been ticking. Define slowly."

"Have I warned you I'm a procrastinator?" Cas was holding on to his control by a fingernail.

"I don't believe you. You're thoughtful, deliberate, delicious."

He surrendered to another kiss.

CHAPTER TEN

Bea couldn't remember being this excited. Ever. She pressed her hand to her belly, where acrobats daily practised a different routine. A weekend away with Cas. A weekend where she could forget work, Jackson, family, mortgages and just enjoy Casildo's company.

My idea of heaven.

Telling her about his dreams and his desire to prove himself to his father had opened another door between them. A shared understanding of obligations to family, of the limitations those obligations placed on other relationships.

He's got a business to establish.

I've got a mortgage to repay.

We've been honest. No harm, no foul.

A discreet, time- and space-limited affair, spectacular and dramatic like a moon flower blossoming overnight. Nature decreed that despite its beauty, the flower didn't bloom again.

No one knew they were sharing this apartment.

He was probably right to move slowly, but Bea was afraid they'd still be moving slowly when it was time for her to go home.

So, on Friday morning, Bea was up, packed and bouncing from foot to foot by the time Casildo said they were good to go. She added a small esky and a box of foodstuffs to her overnight suitcase at the front door.

"I thought we'd stop in Bowral for breakfast." Casildo had returned from loading his gear and was studying her pile. "The Gumnut cake shop is there. Coffee and toast for breakfast, plus we can pick up a supply of nibbles."

"When do you plan to nibble?"

"Morning tea, afternoon tea, supper. I don't often get offered Gumnut cakes." He gestured with his chin. "What have you got, apart from ginger tea?"

"Fruit, some cereal, two cold beers for on arrival."

"You love me." His face lit with his magic smile.

I just might.

It won't hurt if I fall a little, so long as I don't tell anyone.

She'd been bolder last night with her touches, an edge of desperation to her kisses knowing they had so little time together. She yearned for his touch. He'd called a halt.

And she needed him to be one hundred percent with her.

"It's a thank you for organising this, and you'll be tired after the drive."

"No tireder than you. We're sharing the driving. Hour about, and we'll both stay fresh." He hoisted the box and her overnight bag. "We share the driving in our family, don't you?"

"Papá struggles between the old, the new and hard reality. He'd like to earn enough money so Mamá doesn't have to work full-time." *So I don't need to contribute.* "He'd have liked a son."

"Because boys snort, fart and scratch themselves while watching footy with their dads and girls don't?"

"Not having grown up around many boys, you're expanding my education. Is that what you and Hunter do when you're alone?"

"Hunt's a natural gentleman."

So are you.

Everything she'd learned about Casildo proved he had no off switch when it came to his friends. She didn't want him to get some quixotic idea he needed to help her. Not when the price for him would be so high.

She just had to keep her mouth shut for the next two weeks and part friends.

We're friends. His trust was important to her.

"Back to Papá." Bea locked the front door. It was so easy to be with Casildo. He teased, he talked, and he was plain good company. "Driving on family outings was a privilege he claimed for himself. He also loves his car. Cares for it like a newborn. His family didn't have a car when he was a kid."

They argued music as they headed out of Sydney, finally settling on Kasey Chambers. By the time they hit Bowral and the Gumnut café, they'd memorised the words to most tracks on *Wayward Angel* and were loudly belting out the choruses. The café was as good as billed. Casildo bought her French pastries as nibbles. In Albury, he selected an old-fashioned Greek café that served freshly baked stuffed tomatoes and capsicums.

"They're called Yemista," he said.

She drove the next stretch, her focus on the road, although her mind wandered. She'd wondered why Casildo was single. Mo had given her an opening, and Casildo had answered her questions. Monique's lies had hurt him on so many levels, making real his fear of disappointing his father, but also making him doubt his desirability as a lover.

I hate that idea.

He needs to banish the disappointment he sees in his father's eyes.

He also deserves to know that I want him for himself. That he's sexy and just plain good. I want to leave him with happy memories to replace the sense of failure left by Monique.

We've agreed we're not looking long-term.

I'm not available. He's not available.

And let's face it, he wants to get me naked as much as I want it.

The real casualty might be her friendship with Casildo.

Except, he remembered what Bea had been wearing the day they'd met and could describe it accurately. She'd been nervous about attending her first big industry function and had worn her tiger jacket to give her confidence.

Casildo had spoken to her, and where he made contact, others followed. She'd forgotten that. He'd eased her path in thousands of small ways over the years. A nod from across a room, a raised eyebrow when someone expressed surprise that a campaign had flopped when everyone else had known it would. A gentle friendship.

He'd been here all the time.

She'd been aware of him all the time. Always forbidden fruit. Never more so than now.

Lost in her thoughts, she was surprised to see road signs saying they'd hit the outskirts of Bendigo and needed to slow down.

"Pull over here. I'll drive this last bit. The address is in my phone, and you can check out the sights."

Ten minutes later, he pulled up outside a graceful two-story caramel brick building. "That's the main complex. The accommodation is a series of small bungalows."

"It looks gorgeous. And there's a park and lake across the street." Bea pushed open her door and climbed out, letting the scented air and sound of birdcalls welcome her, looking everywhere at once. She didn't get out of Sydney often enough.

"Lake Weeroona. Remember, I've been here before." He joined her. "We don't have long, but it'll be nice to see some of the sights. The show is at the Racecourse, so a bit further out of town."

"This is a fabulous idea." Bea rested her head on his shoulder. "Thank you."

"Let's head inside and get the keys."

Trailing Casildo up the path, Bea played with her

favourite fantasy. The holiday unit might have separate bedrooms, but she'd chosen an old shoe-string strapped satin petticoat, trimmed in milk chocolate lace at her breasts as her nightdress. She'd just walk past him on the way to bed ...

They'd made out every night this week, and his increasingly passionate goodnight kisses had left her hot, wanting and pleasuring herself before she could sleep. Last night, it had taken monumental self-discipline to unravel herself from him and disappear into a separate room The hard ridge of flesh nestled between them before they'd parted hinted that he was as aroused as she was. She hadn't choreographed all her moves for the weekend, but at this moment no one in the world knew where they were. Freedom was wickedly intoxicating.

A sign in the lobby advised them to press for assistance if no one was at the front desk.

A woman arrived hard on the sound of the buzzer. "Hello. Welcome to Bendigo."

"We've got a booking. Name of Ramirez." Casildo handed over the slip of paper.

"I'm guessing you're here for the Lost Trades Fair. Is it your first time?" The woman busied herself crosschecking details.

"I've been before, but it's new for Beatriz. We're really looking forward to it."

"You've got lovely weather for it. Two nights' accommodation for two people." The woman held up a keycard. "We've had to swap rooms for you. A plumbing problem we discovered this morning." She smiled her apology. "But the replacement is our best room. The wedding suite. It's upstairs in this main building and is the only unit we have free."

Casildo turned to her and held up his hands in surrender.

A giggle tickled Bea's throat and came out as a half-snort, then a full-throated laugh. "We'll take it."

"Are you out of your mind?" He hissed.

Bea slipped her hand under his elbow and drew him to one side of the room. "What's the alternative? What's your accommodation Plan B?"

"I don't have one."

"Then this is it." She turned back to the counter.

He grabbed her elbow this time and lowered his forehead to hers. "You know what this means?"

"You can say no." She giggled. "Again."

The bemused motel manager was holding up the keycard. "Will you be taking the room?"

"Yes. Please." Casildo accepted the card, then drew Beatriz back out of earshot of the clearly interested manager. "This isn't how I planned to seduce you."

"But you had a plan."

"Yes. No. I'm trying to think for both of us."

"Then don't. I might have my own plans." She nudged his shoulder. "How about you go collect our bags, while I use the bathroom?"

He looked at her as if unsure, but she made a shooing gesture with her hand. In the bathroom, Bea found what she needed, and was waiting in the lobby when he returned with their overnight bags.

"Let's go have a look at the honeymoon suite, check out their definition of luxury." She took her bag.

"Have you ever stayed in a honeymoon suite?"

She raised an eyebrow.

"What? You might have had an offer like this before."

"Have you?"

"This is a first for me. What do you reckon we'll find?"

"Is this another of your 'five questions before we arrive' games?"

He took her arm. "Guess."

"The entryway, even the guest bathroom in the lobby are a bit oldie-worldie English. A few too many frills for my taste, although some of the fabrics are traditional prints."

"So bog awful?" He grinned.

"Probably lots of pillows."

"I can work with that."

"Work with that, how?" She paused at the bottom of the stairs.

"That's a surprise for later." He caught her elbow. "One more thing."

She turned to him. "I'm not offering to sleep on the floor."

"We have to talk."

"We will." Bea caught his free hand, a way to settle her nerves. "I want to know what you think of the soft furnishings. A professional view, then we might try the bed." She led him to the second floor. "Purely in the interests of assessing mattress quality, fabric and thread count of sheets. I wonder if they have a pillow menu? I imagine you have certain standards where resting your naked body is concerned."

"Right now, all I can think of is your naked body," he growled.

She leaned toward him and ran a hand down his chest to hover above his abdomen. "You're about to get a chance to test imagination against reality, and you might be disappointed—" She was babbling to disguise her growing nervousness.

"I could never be disappointed."

"I haven't finished." Bea stopped at the top of the stairs, checking room numbers. "Looks like we're down that way. We might be duds in bed together. You know, no chemistry."

"You're determined I'll find out." He walked the length of the hall, keyed in his card, pushed the door wide and gestured for her to precede him.

She sashayed past him, patting his cheek on the way. "Only if you're willing, Casildo. I'll need to be very clear that you want this as much as I do. I don't take unwilling lovers to my bed."

In seconds, Bea registered a double tester bed—*who still had them?*—patterned wallpaper, scatter rugs on a polished wood floor, and heavy drapes tied to one side of the bay window hosting a cushioned seat. Stifling another giggle, part jitters and part sheer delight, she set her bag down before heading for the window. The bed occupied a third of the room—hard to avoid—but she focused on the window. Once there, she stared out at the park.

I want this. With Casildo. Only Casildo.

"What a lovely outlook."

"Cute," Casildo muttered.

She turned, her expression schooled to innocence.

"Pretending not to see the elephant in the room." He was staring at the huge old-fashioned bed, of a type she'd thought had disappeared with central heating.

She peered more closely at the pattern on the bed drapes. "Oh, that!" She waved an airy hand. "Aren't they gumnuts, not elephants?"

He snorted.

She toed off her boots and clambered onto the bed, patting the spot beside her. "Come tell Aunty Bea what's troubling you."

"You're not an aunt yet." He ditched his shoes and positioned himself beside her, thumping the pillows so he could get comfortable. "It's medieval."

"Sharing a bed probably started long before medieval times."

"Ha ha."

"Give me your professional assessment," she said, snuggling under his arm and resting her head on his chest. They hadn't got as far as snuggling in a bed before now. Chairs, sofas, but her honourable hero had resisted all invitations to strip down.

"Renovated maybe a decade ago. Wallpaper is an old William Morris design, based on Acanthus leaves and their colours as they age and change. It's a classic and I like it, but we're in small country town Australia, and I'd go for Aussie colours and designs. She's overdone it as well, picking it up in the rugs, doona cover and cushions. At least the curtains and lampshades are block colours."

"Is she trying to create a particular mood?" Bea walked her fingers down his ribcage.

"Wealth, old-fashioned comfort, designs that have stood the test of time," he mused.

"She might see comfort and durability as good emblems for marriage?" Reaching his midriff, Bea let her fingers drift toward his belt buckle.

"Except it's a mishmash." He caught her hand and kissed her fingertips. "William Morris was nineteenth century, an outstanding designer for his times. The tester bed started centuries earlier and was redesigned multiple times. When people stopped sleeping on the floor around the fire, the curtains were designed to keep heat in."

"And here I thought the rugs were intended to invite us to roll around in the autumn leaves."

"I'm guessing it's not to your taste?"

With her head on his chest, she let the rumble of his voice echo in her ear, comforting, steady. This was what she wanted.

He wriggled his way a bit lower on the pillows. "What do you think?"

Bea hesitated. He was letting her lead—exhilarating, arousing and a bit scary. They'd built anticipation to an unbearable edge, now nerves threatened to overwhelm her.

I've never had a lover like Casildo before.

"Maybe the bed linen's more recent? Nothing survives the wash cycle of a commercial laundry for long," she said, pushing herself to a sitting position, before bouncing on the bed. "The mattress seems pretty good. No squeaking. We'll be good when we turn out the lights."

"Make no mistake, the lights won't be off when I make love to you."

"When." Am I ready for what his sultry gaze promises?

She flipped onto her knees and pushed the cushions and excess pillows onto the floor, her heart hammering, and her insides liquid fire.

"What are you doing?"

"Checking the sheets. Can you tell the thread count without reading the label?"

"I'd have a good idea." He placed his hand on hers, rolling to his knees. "To repeat a friend of mine, I don't take unwilling lovers to bed. You can change your mind at any time. No need for nerves."

"I'm not nervous." *Yes, I am* "Well, maybe a bit."

"No need." He linked his fingers with hers. "I reckon we've got the kissing bit sorted."

She smiled. "You're right."

"Then, please, Beatriz, for the sake of my sanity ..." He pressed her hand to his chest.

"You want me?"

"Very much." His grin was tender.

Tension flowed out of her, leaving a gooey mashup of desire and affection. This was Casildo.

Leaning forward, Bea brushed her lips across his, her moan involuntary. She drew back, cupping his jaw. Her nights had been filled with dreams, the smooth texture of his lips, the edge of his teeth when he grazed her bottom lip, his teasing tongue testing their resolve to keep their touches on the barely controlled side of abandon.

Then his mouth was on hers. Just his mouth. An invitation, a promise of more, and blood heated her skin. This kiss hinted that abandon was within reach, and so much sweeter for the anticipation that had gone before. She trailed her fingers up his neck, enjoying its elegance, then moved higher, across his sharp cheekbones to tangle her fingers in the thick hank of hair falling forward across his forehead. So many luscious textures. Dreams and reality collided. Heaven.

Her breath hitched when he slid his arms around her, one hand stroking her spine, the other gripping one buttock and pulling her flush against him. When he insinuated his thigh between her legs, she leaned back, her vision blurred but wanting to give him the words. "Yes, Casildo, please."

She rubbed herself against his thigh, the brush of denim against denim heightening her arousal. He soothed with a nuzzle to her throat.

"We have all the time in the world."

"And still I want to rush, to ravish you," she murmured. *I'm afraid I'll lose you if we don't love now.*

"Easy, sweetheart. We're not in a hurry."

"I'm in a hurry." She pulled him closer.

"I can see that." He ran his hands over her cotton-covered breasts. "Let's undo your buttons."

"I want your shirt off first." Exhilarating to issue commands to a lover.

Casildo wasn't intimidated by her taking charge, hauling his shirt over his head to drop it beside the bed.

"You're gorgeous." She ran her hands over his chest. "Anyone would think you work out."

"Good genes. You should see Hunt's."

She giggled. "So I'm guessing you're an active cheer squad at those TV football nights."

"Join me one night?"

"Don't mind if I do. Someone had to keep Dad company."

He pulled her close for a friendly cuddle. "You say the sexiest things."

She placed her hand on his belt buckle. "Let's do some sexy things."

"Someone needs to lose her shirt first." He undid a few buttons, but his fingers faltered. "Too slow. Raise your arms." His voice ragged, he pulled her shirt up until her hands were imprisoned in the folds of fabric, and he was stretched forward, his bare chest brushing her bra-clad breasts. He easily held her in position with one hand. With his other, he pushed her bra up, bending to suckle.

"You taste like that first sip of hot chocolate, hot and sweet." He sounded awed. "How do you do that?"

"Now, I can finally touch you." She sighed, ignoring his question.

But having ditched her shirt, he slid down the bed, unclipped her bra and tossed it aside. When he palmed one breast, she cried out.

"You like that." His gaze heated, and he repeated the action with her other breast, laving the nipple until both stood erect.

They'd leapfrogged what they'd allowed themselves in Anna's apartment. Touching through clothes was the furthest they'd gone. Hot, heavy kisses, leaving them both aroused, but knowing more was within reach. Bea had been weak with wanting, while Casildo had urged caution.

"We've wasted so much time," she murmured.

"Not anymore."

"Roll over," she instructed, moving with him until she straddled his upper thighs. "You have the sexiest body. Tonight, you're all mine."

"I have injuries from becoming Hunt's blood brother."

"Show me."

He pointed to the thin scar that stretched under his ribcage.

"I'll kiss it better."

But she wanted to kiss the hurt he carried deep inside him better. For now, she started with an old scar from a game between friends, moved from there to his nipples, sucking and licking by turns, growing bolder hearing his groans of pleasure, seeing his clenched fists. Then she rested her cheek on his heart while tracing another heart on his chest.

"See, all better."

With a roar, he flipped her over, crouching above her on all fours. "Decision time."

"No one knows we're here, Cas."

"Maha," he blurted. "I told her you were coming with me."

"And I'm guessing Maha has kept your secrets for years, just like you've kept hers. This is for us. A moment in time." One hand cupped his jaw as he poised above her.

"You're sure?"

"You make me sure." She loved the care he took, checking to see that this was her choice, unable to remember the last time her wishes had come first.

"Hell, my heart's hammering in my chest." He pulled her palm against his chest. "I want you."

"I want you too." Telling him was a different kind of risk, one she hadn't taken in a long time. Maybe ever.

"Make love with me."

Bea should have anticipated a mutual lovemaking, rather than an exercise in power or ego. No other lover had prepared her for those words, and they took her over a precipice, into the unknown. "I'd love that."

"I will too. There's only one problem."

"Only one?" She stroked a hand over his pants. "You feel very ready."

His hand covered hers. "When I said I planned to seduce you, I meant I've fantasised. Often. But I don't want you to take a step you'll regret."

"Can you see regrets?"

"No, and I'm an idiot. I decided the best protection was no protection. No rubbers."

"Oh dear." She put a hand across her mouth, then laughed up at him. "There's a vending machine in the lobby bathroom."

"Right."

"I noticed on the way in."

"Thank you, Jaddatee."

"Thank you, Grandma. That's an unusual blessing."

"I credit her with bequeathing me all the good things in life. The lobby's better than the nearest market. I'll be right back." He made to get off the bed.

"I picked up a few strips while you were out getting the bags," she admitted, gesturing to the handbag she'd dropped beside the bed.

"Did you now?" He resumed his crouch above her, his hand trailing down her midriff, over her jeans and cupping her mons.

"I thought you might bring some. Why didn't you, Cas?"

"I didn't want to presume."

With that, she fell all the way in love.

He didn't want to presume. He didn't want to hurt her. He'd armed her to fight Jackson. He prioritised her wants and needs. He'd given her this weekend, and she refused to waste it.

His cupped hand pressing gently between her upper legs was electrifying, sensations zipping along synapses at the speed of light making her body hum.

"Presume all you want." She was finding it hard to form coherent sentences with his knee nudging her knees apart. She whimpered. "Because then I can presume too. And either one of us can call a halt."

"I won't be calling a halt," he murmured. "I've waited too long for this."

"Neither will I."

Not tonight. Bea would struggle to call a halt at the end of the month when she had to give him up. She wasn't strong enough to call a halt now, when it might make a difference.

CHAPTER ELEVEN

Beatriz moved beneath Cas in sinuous waves, luminous in her pleasure. And she was here with him, a man who'd be living in relative poverty while he launched his business.

She made him feel invincible and cherished.

When has a woman ever made me feel cherished?

"Then let's get rid of a few more clothes." Cas wanted to tease her and ravish her simultaneously. She was joy and passion, brains and compassion.

"You're lovely. I should have told you that before." He'd flipped the moment to seriousness, and she withdrew slightly.

What had she said? "*A fling.*" The word made no sense in this moment.

He crab-walked backward until he was near her ankles. "I want to do you slowly."

"One of us might go mad if I have to wait much longer."

He laughed. "These are more tights than jeans. I'll have to pull them off. Lift your hips"

She lifted, thrusting her pelvis toward him.

"Playing with fire, Beatriz." He got his hands in the back waistband and tugged the jean-like tights down, bringing her knickers with them. Bending forward, he rested his cheek against her mons. "I like the way you smell." He nosed against her. "You smell a bit like gingerbread—all aroused and mine."

"I thought touch was your preferred sense." Her hands tangled in his hair, her voice croaky.

"With you, I want to touch, taste, listen"—he loved her little pants of pleasure—"watch"—to see her eyes go soft with passion—"and act. Starting now." He stared at her nakedness. "You're stunning. Don't shake your head. Believe me."

With his heart racing, his blood heating to boiling, and a roaring in his ears, Cas released her ankles, tugged the trousers over her feet and tossed them aside, before shucking his own. His erection bounced free.

"Someone's pleased to see me."

Grasping one foot, he flexed her leg until her thighs fell open. He tempted her with small nibbles, light kisses up the inside of her leg, absorbing her moans, watching her writhe on the bed.

"You're touching yourself."

"I can't reach you," she whimpered.

"Are you wet, Beatriz?"

She slid a finger inside herself then pressed it to his lips. He inhaled her scent, then opened his mouth and sucked.

"Would you like me to bring you off? Take the edge off, so we can take our time," he whispered against her ear.

"I want us together the first time," she breathed.

And he handed the remainder of his heart into her keeping. Emotional intimacy. This was what love felt like. Orgasms were easy, even multiple orgasms if you paced yourself, and he planned to pace himself tonight, but this moment couldn't be repeated.

"The strip's in the side pocket of my bag."

He slid his hand down, grabbed the foils and tore one off.

"Wanna be on top?" Cas wouldn't be able to manage much more conversation with his cock throbbing and his head about to explode.

"Hips up." She pulled a pillow beneath her hips as she spoke. "Love me, Casildo."

I will.

He nudged his cock toward her, exulting when her slick wetness cloaked his tip. Cas drew back, then moved forward again, slight increments while he kept his gaze on her, arousal spilling into a building tension. Going deeper, he brushed a finger over her clitoris, while keeping up a steady rhythm.

"Harder. Faster," she stammered, her breath ragged when Cas upped the speed.

She was close, and Cas adjusted his tempo, listening for the slap of skin against skin, feeling the slick of sweat down his spine, and he wanted to hold all those senses in his head, to remember loving Beatriz this first time. She used her hand to guide him to a slightly different angle. Her eyes closed, then shot wide open, and he gave a last thrust and let go.

"Yes," she gave a half-scream, half-moan, but his body was already unravelling, draining him.

I've just been loved, he thought.

So this is what it's like.

He gathered Beatriz close. Tonight was for more holding and loving, but soon he'd convince her they were right together.

No. That wasn't the deal.

Except holding her comforted him to his toes, while stirring the desire he'd told himself was a figment of proximity, the fabrics she wore, and her soft giggle when he trailed a hand down her spine, bending her toward him. He pushed recriminations from his mind. Her giggles melted into soft moans when he started kissing her.

He loved kissing her.

What have I done?

* * *

Truly, could the world go from magical to the pits in twenty-four hours?

After they'd surfaced on Friday night, Casildo had called intermission and insisted they try one of the restaurants in town. She had vague memories of red-and-white-checked tablecloths, candles in chianti bottles and divine flavours. Clearer in her memory was them sitting hip to hip, staring into each other's eyes, and him letting her convince him to go home early.

On Saturday, they'd explored the markets together, visiting every stall, holding hands, stopping occasionally to share kisses, unable to wipe the smiles off their faces. On Sunday morning, they'd made love until they were scrambling to meet the deadline for checkout, giggling as they packed the car.

Sunday night, they'd slept, wrapped in each other's arms.

Monday brought reality.

Beatriz hesitated outside the apartment door, her forehead resting on the wood. She didn't want to bring trouble home, but she was so angry about Jackson, she wasn't sure she could keep it to herself. She sighed, and the door opened, tumbling her into Casildo's arms.

"What's wrong?" He put an arm around her shoulders, drawing her down the hall, into the living room and guiding her to her favourite corner of the sofa. He perched on the coffee table so they were knee to knee.

"Nothing." She tried to deflect him.

"You look so woebegone, so"—he paused—"defeated. That's not like you."

Bea wanted him to lift her into his lap and tell her he'd kiss it better, but that solved nothing. And it wasn't his problem.

"Want some tea? Ginger, black, a glass of wine, something stronger." He took her hand. "Anna must have something stronger hidden somewhere."

"Brandy for her Christmas cakes."

"I thought her cooking skills were on the non-existent side of basic." He was trying to make her smile.

"She makes an effort at Christmas. Her parents didn't."

"Rebellion. It pops up in the strangest ways."

He'd made her smile, and he deserved to know that. "Thanks."

"What happened?"

"I'm making a mountain out of a molehill."

"Not usually."

"Jackson has asked for a rearrangement of teams now he's management. He wants me on his team. Only me. We're going to spearhead a new initiative, spark new ideas, manage branding differently."

"Who told you?"

"He did. I can't afford to lose my job," she wailed, and Casildo could make of that what he wanted. It wasn't an absolute admission that her entire pay packet was committed to her family, but it was the closest she'd come.

"Any official announcement?"

"Jackson sidled up to me and whispered in my ear." She shivered.

"Did he touch you?"

"Not this time."

"Without an official announcement, it might be wishful thinking on his part. What are you going to do?"

"Do?" She blinked at him.

"Yes. What are you going to do to prevent Jackson the Barbarian from making your life a living misery while he feeds off your ideas?" Casildo sounded calm, but his eyes were anything but.

"I can accept it, or I can leave."

"You have other options. Think, Beatriz. There were three people on that recruitment panel. The decision to give the job to Jackson wasn't unanimous. I'm guessing the independent was sucked in by his slick style. Who would have taken your side?"

"The idea of working with Jackson makes my brain

freeze."

"Unfreeze it. Why were you at the Digital Print Show?"

"Martin said he had some ideas for my next steps." Bea frowned. Her boss hadn't given the slightest hint she'd be working with Jackson on projects.

"*Your* next steps. Not yours and Jackson's. Do you think Martin will let you go at a word from Jackson?" He eased a thumb over her furrowed brow.

"I think better when you hold me," she whispered, regretting in that moment all the days and nights of her life he'd be gone.

"I think better when you're in my arms." He switched to the sofa and lifted her onto his lap.

"I'll talk to him. First thing in the morning."

"You sound determined. I like that more than defeated. What will you say?"

She stared at him. "You like that I'm determined and persistent?"

"Essential survival skills in migrant families, especially when you're the eldest." He pressed his forehead to hers. "What will you say? C'mon, it makes sense to workshop it a bit."

"What do you think I should say?" she asked.

"Not gonna catch me with that one. This is your fight. If ever there was a moment for rebellion, it's now. What do you want to say to Martin?"

"That Jackson stole my ideas." She combed Casildo's unruly curl back from his forehead.

"Prove it." He smiled at her. "You can prove it, can't you?"

"Yes," she said slowly. "I use passwords. My e-files will have creation and modification dates."

"So how come Jackson got hold of them?"

"I printed a copy. I wanted to take it home, read it in print form."

"And?'

"I put it in my laptop backpack, but when I came back

from a meeting, my backpack had been moved." Bea had dismissed her suspicion. Decided she'd been mistaken, until the independent had asked her question with a smug smirk, and Bea's plans had unravelled.

"That's pretty flimsy evidence. Was Jackson near your desk when you came back?"

"At the next desk." She stared over Cas's shoulder, trying to recall the scene.

"You don't fight dirty, which is a handicap."

"Neither do you, Cas." She tugged on his recalcitrant curl.

"Yeah, but I'm not all soft and gooey on the inside like you." He grinned. "Okay, let's say I'm buying the possibility. What's suspicious about him being at the next desk?"

"He's been chatting up my new intern Rachel for weeks. I texted to tell Rachel my meeting had ended earlier than expected, so she and I could bring forward our training session."

"Are you saying she's his accomplice?' he asked, drawing circles at the base of her spine.

"Rachel's besotted. Maybe enough to let him steal a report from my backpack, copy it, or read it?" Bea paused. "That doesn't ring true. She's besotted, but not a complete idiot. He must have spun her a plausible excuse. Said I'd asked him to check out the report."

"So, if Martin spoke to this intern privately, she might confirm your story?" His hand paused.

"Don't stop." She thought about what Casildo had said, while he resumed his steady caress of her lower back. "Yes."

"How did you find out he'd stolen your ideas?"

"The independent asked a supplementary question after I talked about my ideas in the interview. She asked if I'd talked to Jackson about his ideas?"

"You were furious and hurt by his betrayal."

"Damn right." The combination had crippled her. "I didn't know how to fight back."

Cas kissed her temple. "Not very professional of her."

"But it explained the result. She believed Jackson was the innovator, not me."

"He deserves to be kicked in the cods, but you're too polite for that, so what's your price?"

Bea rested her cheek against his chest, silent while she figured angles. "If Martin believes me, I've won. I won't be assigned to Jackson. Martin will make the case to higher management. Jackson won't rise higher in the company, and they might let him go."

"That's a good outcome, isn't it?"

"He might need the job too. I don't know his personal circumstances."

"Are you sure you have the ruthlessness to run your own business?" he teased.

"You aren't ruthless, and you want to run your own business."

"I've been known to be ruthless."

"No, you haven't." She pressed her forehead to his. "It's one of the reasons I … like you so much." She'd nearly said love.

No harm, no foul. Remember?

"Thanks for helping with this. You're a good man, Cas. I admire that about you."

"Since we're comfortable here, why don't we admire each other a bit more?" He nuzzled behind her ear.

"What do you have in mind?"

He flipped open a button, then slipped a hand inside her shirt and under her bra. "I thought I'd start here."

"Yes, please."

Making love to him was easy. Loving him was even easier. Just dangerous.

* * *

Cas stepped out of Mo's office the following afternoon and texted Beatriz:

On my way.

Her reply pinged back almost instantly.

All good.

He wasn't used to letting anyone know he was on his way home. Yet, it was his first instinct after farewelling Mo. Liking that she responded was another new experience. Flatmates. Was it just politeness? Her turn to cook dinner, so he let her know his movements?

It's more than that.

I'm going home.

You idiot.

It's not your home.

But, it was the kind of home he'd like to have. Shared chores, sexy companion, someone who believed in his dreams.

Walking up the stairs to the apartment, the smell of Thai curry wafted under the front door, sharpening his appetite. Beatriz in the kitchen wearing his apron *Real men cook* sharpened another appetite, and they were both pretty happy about how that was working out.

Honey, I'm home.

"Hi."

She turned toward him, her mouth spreading into a smile. Delight, welcome—he could walk into that smile every day and die a happy man. She stepped closer to kiss him. His hands automatically reached for her hips to draw her closer.

She eased back. "Meet you in the dining room. I'll bring the beers."

He wanted to stay, to sweep her into his arms, and just hold her. Living with her, he appreciated her on a different level to the professional. Despite the challenges she was currently dealing with, like her sisters and Jackson Smithers, she was content. He remembered Monique had never been content, and knew a moment's sympathy for a woman who'd never be happy. Bea found happiness in small moments, and Cas found that side of her personality irresistible.

"I'll change."

Cas's patterns had started to change before he and Beatriz had become lovers. On nights when he was home first, he'd started listening for her arrival. Like a kid waiting for a treat. He'd started leaving work earlier since moving in with Beatriz. A holiday from his real world. Better now they were lovers.

If it was his night to cook, she'd pop her head into the kitchen and sniff the air, wanting to guess what he was making before he told her. He played the same game when she cooked. Harmless, friendly, the sort of thing flatmates comfortable with each other would do. They'd fallen into a comfortable living routine. That had never been a feature of his previous relationships.

It can't last.

I can't let it last.

They were intimate in a way he'd never imagined. And from the moment he'd met her, he'd guessed deep down this might happen, and had kept contact with Beatriz work-focused as a result. Better now he'd come to terms with his disillusion about Monique. Beatriz deserved better. Pouring all his money and time into a new business put limits on what he could offer her.

Except Beatriz hadn't changed. A fling. She never alluded to the future, especially a shared future, and it was starting to niggle at him. She was right that they'd agreed on a fling, but his heart kept asking *Why not*?

"Take your time. Dinner's about twenty minutes."

"Give me five."

Shucking his work gear for jeans and a tee, Cas joined her in the loungeroom.

She handed him a beer. "Cheers."

He'd shared all his secrets with her, including his fear of having let his dad down, and somehow skinned another layer off his protective skin. She'd shared first, and having the self-contained Beatriz Gomez admit she was afraid of Jackson ambushing her triggered all the protective instincts he usually reserved for family.

With Beatriz he didn't feel exposed or besieged. He searched for a word that fitted. Safe. A boring word, but safety in a lover's arms had eluded him for much of his adult life. He was too easy a target for his family's perceived wealth.

It's not real, Cas. She agreed to an affair.

"Have you heard from Mo?"

"Mo's interested."

She clapped her hands.

"I'm talking about spending every dime I'm likely to earn for years, and you're cheering?"

"I'm excited."

Her excitement seemed to rise in direct proportion to his progress toward setting up his business. She remembered the rules even when he was floating in a sex-drugged haze. He couldn't believe she only wanted the sex.

"Yeah. I'm pleased too. But we've got a way to go yet." Lots of those pesky logistical details that weren't his forte.

"Based on the plans he outlined to me—and I'm not breaking business confidentiality here—he wants to offer a service to any large or small business interested in his products, and despite my best efforts, he's still leaning toward Sunshine Superman, although he is considering Ally's Prints after his daughter."

"Terrible habit, naming a business after families. Dad resisted the pressure to call The Hariri building Hariri and Son, but Ally's Prints is a tribute rather than assuming a dynasty."

"What do you think your father's business should be called? Is it the dynastic element of it that worries you?"

"I hated those endless conversations between Dad and his business associates when I was a kid. I wished the earth would swallow me. One of them would always finish with 'and when's the sign for Hariri and Son going up?' If anything, it should read Hariri and Sons. Better still, Hariri and Children—a fitting tribute to moving the Hariri family halfway around the world for a different kind of future. Hariri and Family sounds even better. That makes it intergenerational, and allows for any variations in surnames."

"Suggest it. Your family likes to break traditions." Her smile was full of mischief.

"I just might. What about yours?"

"I think they're completely Australian and have absorbed all the local customs, then something happens, and I'm faced with decisions their parents might have made in Chile. And you're trying to distract me. Is nature where you get your inspiration?"

"Colours and patterns fascinate me. I was surrounded by them at Jaddatee's. She bought books when she saw I was interested, and crayons and watercolours, even oils. Although they were never my thing."

"You realise you need a name and a brand for yourself."

"Mo and I traded for a while. We'd workshopped what we wanted to be known for, tested it out."

"Tested what out? I want to know everything."

"I designed. He printed fabrics."

"Right. You just designed independently in your attic and then handed them over. He chose fabric, colour variations, production quantity, price, outlets, what?"

"We approached a company with the design. If we got interest, then we produced based on the order."

"How did you choose a company to approach?"

"There aren't that many that do high-end, unique designs using sustainable dyes and fabrics."

"So you built up a clientele?"

"We were building a clientele. Then he married Evie."

"Did you continue alone?"

"Yeah. I have. Not so much since Nick Richardson appeared on the scene."

"Getting information out of you is harder than getting trade secrets from Anna."

"You're competitors."

"You and I aren't. At least on this. Mo is interested in pairing up with you again."

"He's exploring ways and means. He's got the machinery; he knows where to find the relevant suppliers for dyes and fabrics. He's started to put out feelers for workers. But he's proceeding slowly. And he wouldn't just print my designs. So, essentially, we could have two separate businesses co-located. Finding the right location at the right price is the challenge."

"Do you have any ideas about that? And yes, I'm prodding because possible premises haven't come up in our conversations so far."

"Prodding is good." He stared at her. "And not really is the answer."

"Because you spend every spare moment on designs?"

"I've nailed my criteria."

She looked sceptical.

"Shows I need to work harder at this business stuff. Dad or Hunt or even Maha would have a short list of sites by now."

"What name did you and Mo use?"

"Casmo Fabric for Unique Interiors."

"I like the unique part of it."

"I kept it even though he wasn't doing the printing anymore."

"Because you liked working with Mo?"

"Yeah, and even though he had his hands full when we dissolved our partnership, he said to call him any time. I forgot that."

"You're lucky you didn't forget your own name with Monique and Nick Richardson after you."

"You're the brand expert. Suggest something."

"I'll give it some thought. Now, tell me, what's holding you back from looking for premises?"

"You see too much." He grabbed the back of his neck. "I'm worried that the experience has kicked Dad off his axis, but I'm also worried that I'm imagining things."

"Talk to him."

"I'm waiting for Hunter. He has a better understanding of the market, of how Dad would be feeling after such a knock."

"You're underestimating yourself. You have more natural empathy than Hunter. If you're picking up distracted vibes, I'd say your dad has got something on his mind. But don't give up your plans. They're good plans, and you do exceptional work."

The buzzer from the stove sounded.

"If you set the table, I'll bring dinner through."

Cas stayed on the sofa after she left. Beatriz inspired him to design and made him feel his dreams could be real. He wanted to hold her, to love her, but it wasn't fair to ask her to take a risk on him. Was it?

Al'ama. Maybe they needed to change the rules.

He rose and set the table, then helped carry the meals from the kitchen to the table.

"I've been wondering about your competition. I haven't found a lot in my searches, but do many companies use organic textiles?"

"A growing number. Mo and I decided we could work with that for a start, although the samples we took them were on organic wool and cotton using natural dyes and printing methods. Silk's harder to source, but becoming more available."

"I've never heard of organic silk." She sounded fascinated, the perfect sounding board for his ideas.

"It's a much smaller part of the market. It's called peace silk, and you can source it from India."

"How do you know it's legit?"

"Good question." He imagined she asked insightful questions of clients every day, making sure whatever marketing plan she crafted was truthful as well as credible. "There are certification organisations."

"That's a large part of why you two wanted your own business, isn't it? The right to source the textiles as well as design and print them."

"It's been my dream for as long as I can remember." And that was the honest truth. "This is probably my last chance."

CHAPTER TWELVE

A week since their weekend away, Beatriz was still pinching herself. She and Casildo had made love in every room in the apartment, even the hall! She was amazed at herself. She was insatiable, as if all the passion in her soul had been waiting for Casildo.

He spent every night in her bed, seduced her with slow, lazy thrusts until she screamed his name. They held hands in the kitchen, cuddled on the sofa, whispered nothings to each other and giggled at memories of the various functions where they'd crossed paths in the last few years.

In her heart she was sure, but she hadn't used the *L* word. It was far too dangerous.

He looked at her sometimes as if about to raise something serious, like what next? And she distracted him. She was searching for the right words to tell him the truth, hampered because she could imagine the disillusion in his eyes.

A fling. All I promised was a fling. I'm lying to him, by omission. I have to find the right moment to tell him the truth.

Bea disentangled herself from Casildo's arms when her phone pinged. She grabbed it off the bedside table. "That's Mamá."

"She can't see us." Casildo's eyes were closed, but his arm, still wrapped around her waist, grounded her.

"Don't be too sure. She's got second sight and mystical powers."

"Then she'll see you're all flushed and have a naked man in your bed." A smile curved his mouth.

"She's inviting us for dinner." Bea froze, uncertain of her next move. "Tonight."

"Then wave to her, say yes, and tell her you're currently busy." His mouth covered her nipple.

The light suckle echoed to her toes, making her fingers tremble as she typed *Yes*. She groaned and dropped the phone.

"That wasn't so hard, was it?" He rose on his knees to straddle her body.

She stroked the length of his cock. "Looks hard to me."

He laughed.

"What's the signal for *Get out now*?" Casildo glanced at her, then refocused on the road.

Bea turned to stare at his profile. Even his profile made her heart beat a little faster. She wasn't sure if he was trying to make her nervous or reassure her. "There is no signal."

"Okaaay. A friendly gathering. What are my topics?"

"You and Maha may have workshopped topics before she introduced Antonio to your parents. But this is different."

This has to be different because we have no future.

"You're the one who said your mother sized up every male as a potential son-in-law. She probably needs to focus since there are five of you."

"Two are married."

"That leaves three." He sent her a sideways look. "I can wax lyrically and at length about Hunter. They've met Hunt, haven't they?"

"Yes," she said.

Do we need a set of innocuous topics?

"So where does that leave us?"

"Not sharing Anna's apartment," she admitted.

"Ships that pass in the night?" he sounded disgruntled.

"Friends?" She held her breath.

You promised we'd always be friends.

She didn't say the words, but he was silent so long, Bea thought she'd black out. Then he seemed to haul himself in.

"I've got a few school stories that might work. You know, the old everyone-looked-at-my-lunch-because-it-was-different."

"Empanadas were a hit."

"The Chilean equivalent of a meat pie?" Casildo pulled into the kerb.

"The car's missing," Bea whispered, her gaze scanning the street around them.

"Why are you whispering? Does your mother have supersonic hearing as well?"

"She does, but it's odd the car's missing when they invited us for dinner."

"Could she have hidden it out the back?" he asked. A ridiculous question when the house sprawled across the block with a car port at the front.

"Now, you're crediting her with levitation skills." Bea was hyperventilating for no reason.

"Do you think she's out collecting the rest of the family?"

"I hope not. She just said come for dinner and bring Casildo."

"But at a minimum, this is Mrs. G., Mr. G. and the two demons."

"You will not call them that at dinner."

"I'll try very hard not to. Tell me their names."

"Elisa, but she prefers Lisa, and Francesca, but she only answers to Fran."

"Wow, where's the *A* to tidy up that alphabetical list of names?"

She glanced at him to discover he was smiling.

"Mamá is Antonella."

"I won't reveal any secrets, Beatriz."

She took another risk, leaning forward to kiss him. Not a casual kiss, but a hold-em-down-until-they give-in kind of kiss. If anyone was looking out of windows, so be it. She couldn't keep him, but she'd take every scrap of joy from being with him while she could.

"Al'ama." He placed her hand on his groin. "We might wait a second or two before we go in or everyone will think my brain's in my pants."

"Ready?"

"I wasn't ready for you, Beatriz. No, that's the wrong word. I wasn't expecting you."

"C'mon, tiger. I'll take you in."

Bea unlocked the front door. The house smelled of home, the flowers her mother always had on the hall table. Mostly from their garden, but occasionally store-bought or a present. Her daughters knew flowers were always welcome as a present or an apology. With six women living together, there was often a need for an apology. Bea discovered that the few short weeks at Anna's apartment had made her reluctant to be peacemaker anymore.

"Someone must be home," Casildo whispered. "Dinner smells divine. Chilean?"

"More likely to be Italian. It's a favourite." Bea turned her back on him. "Anyone home?"

Doors banged upstairs, then her two youngest sisters appeared on the upper landing. She noticed the second their sulky expressions shifted to interest and almost laughed. Casildo might not have been expecting her, but her sisters sure didn't expect her to walk in the door with a certifiable hunk. Casildo could be a male model—lean, athletic. One colleague said he reminded her of Virat Kohli, minus the beard and moustache. Her sisters' mouths widened into smiles, and they sauntered downstairs.

"My sisters, Lisa on the left, Fran on the right."

"I didn't hear the door," Lisa said.

"I thought Mamá and Papá were back," offered Fran.

"We are." Her mother pushed through the door behind them. "Papá's just parking the car."

"Did you forget something?" Bea asked. "We could have picked it up."

"Nothing important." Had her mamá just blushed? "We thought we'd be back before you."

Her father arrived seconds after his wife. "Hello, BB." He enfolded her in a hug, the hug that had always made her feel special as a child. She'd climb onto his lap and tell him her troubles, and he'd kiss her and everything would be better.

It was unfair that at this stage of his life, when he should be able to think of retiring, his injury had upended all his plans, his sense of who he was, and his role in the family. In the absence of anyone else, Bea had adopted the provider role.

Releasing her, he turned to Casildo. "Welcome to our home. I'm sorry I didn't meet you last time you called."

"Thanks for the invitation, Mr. Gomez. Dinner smells fabulous," said Casildo.

"Call me Tomas."

"And you'd better call me Antonella," said her conservative Mamá.

"Maybe we can get past the hall. It's a bit crowded here." Bea had a sense of floating in a parallel universe. Her parents had waited months before they'd given her brothers-in-law permission to use their first names.

"Casildo, you go with Papá and Beatriz into the loungeroom. Girls, you can help me with dinner?"

Bemused, Beatriz followed Casildo and Papá. She was normally the sister in the kitchen helping with food for their guests. Had her absence created change?

"Can I get either of you a drink?" her father asked. "Water, wine, a beer. I've got non-alcoholic beer if you'd prefer?"

"Sounds good." Casildo crossed the room to assist her father.

"I'll have a red wine, please, Papá."

"We've got a good Nero d'Avola to go with your mother's meatballs."

"Sounds lovely." She rarely drank at home. She was rarely waited on at home. Is this how her married sisters felt when they visited? Pampered, like guests in their childhood home. I could get used to being pampered, but not waited on hand and foot by her parents.

"How's work?" her papá always asked. "Jackson Smithers giving you any trouble?"

"The barbarian?" She giggled. "That's Casildo's name for him. And I've spoken to my boss Martin privately and told him Jackson stole my ideas. He gave me a fair hearing and said he'd get back to me."

"That's my girl. Was that your idea too, Casildo?"

They hadn't been in the house twenty minutes and they were in murky territory. Bea had expected the questions to come from her mother, instead, Mamá had primed Papá for the cross-examination before dinner.

"Just the nickname," Casildo said easily. "Because we're in the same industry I've met a lot of Beatriz's colleagues. But I'm glad to hear she outed Jackson. He's been starting to get a reputation for sneaky dealings in our circles, hence my nickname for him."

"Maybe I should help Mamá?" Beatriz made to stand.

"Let your sisters do it for a change."

'For a change?' She'd thought that because Papá was largely tied to the lounge chair he hadn't noticed the division of labour in the house.

"Why did you and Mamá have to go out?" Bea asked. Their absence with guests arriving was so out of character, Bea couldn't let it go.

"Some business we've been doing. A few details to finalise." He was matter-of-fact.

"Anything I can help with?" she asked instinctively.

"No, my darling. Your help got us to this point."

Bea opened her mouth to ask more questions, when her mother interrupted, "Dinner's on the table." Her mother stood in the doorway, signalling her father to stop talking.

Plates were passed around, more drinks poured. Her parents sat at either end of the table as they always did. She and Casildo were diagonally opposite. Fran looked like she'd won Lotto, swivelling in her seat to monopolise Casildo.

On her side of the table, Lisa pouted.

Bea leaned sideways to whisper in her sister's ear. "He's a big fan of basketball."

Lisa played for the university team and was an ardent supporter of the state's NBL team. Lisa waited for Fran to take a mouthful of food and seized her chance. "Bea says you like basketball. Sydney Kings are giving a demonstration at Sydney University next Saturday night. Are you going?"

Bea could relax. Her sisters had no interest in Casildo and Bea, merely Casildo.

"I'll be working. You're lucky if you've got a Saturday night off work," Casildo said, while Bea searched the table for something she could throw at him.

"I'm at university. Primary school teaching. I've only got day classes." Lisa fluffed her hair as if that was all the answer needed.

"Oh," he sounded surprised. "All my friends worked part-time at university. It was a rite of passage. Who had the most bog-awful job, although I would have thought hospitality—mixing with lots of different people—would be good prep for teaching. Hunt actually studied part-time. He worked as a full-time builder's labourer at the time."

"Did you work?" Fran's voice was stilted.

"Sure. At a printer's. Had a lot of fun, met new people and got paid for it. I had a scholarship for fees, but it's still expensive. I'm one of four. Big load for my parents."

He was one of four if you counted Hunt. He always counted Hunt. She loved him for that. Not only that. And she couldn't believe that if Raed Hariri had paid some of

Hunter's university fees, he would ever be disappointed in a son as gentle and sensitive as Casildo Hariri.

One day she might be able to tell Casildo she loved him. Telling him now would mess up his dreams and his plans.

Dinner was a ... revelation, from her being treated as a guest, to her parents' informality with Casildo, to her sisters being assigned the clearing of the table and the cleaning up. All the normal routines had been upended in her absence, and she wasn't sure if that was a good or a bad thing. Her parents had even seemed keen to push her out the door.

"Thank you for coming." Her mamá kissed Casildo on the cheek.

Sitting in the car, waiting for Casildo to pull away from the kerb, Bea reflected on that kiss. A welcome to the family when her mamá knew Bea wasn't free to become involved with anyone. Her mamá's uncharacteristic insensitivity hurt.

"Nice girls, your sisters. Pity they're spoilt."

"I should take the blame for some of it." But the pattern had started when Bea was a child, before she understood it was unfair. "I told you, Mamá nearly lost Daniela. She took the government-funded parental leave, but then needed to go back to work."

"She needed your help."

"You said your mum needed Maha's."

"This isn't a competition, Beatriz. I know how migrant families work. How many families work. Work being the critical word. They're here for us to do well, so they sacrifice a lot of their own dreams to see us thrive. It's disrespectful to take that for granted."

How am I going to leave this man?
I'm not ready to move on.
Except, I'm relying on him to do just that.

* * *

Cas allowed himself to savour the contentment for a precious moment. Beatriz was snuggled under his arm, seemingly inhaling the smell of her man after a vigorous round of late afternoon lovemaking. Cas loved that she was gloriously indulgent when they made love, a sensory banquet.

He was finding it harder and harder to think past the coming weekend.

A pit opened in his stomach. He didn't want a break up with Beatriz, pretend or otherwise, but all of Beatriz's actions in the last few days, including dinner at her parents, suggested she was withdrawing from him publicly. Why so desperate to tell her parents they weren't dating.

Not privately. She initiated sex at every opportunity. Like this afternoon. Made love to him as if she couldn't get enough of him. With the kind of desperation suggesting each day or night might be their last.

That's what you agreed, bro.

"What are you thinking?" she asked drowsily.

"Probably the same thing you're thinking."

"They'll be home tomorrow. What are we going to tell them?"

"I'm going to tell Hunt I've been sharing this apartment with you for the past four weeks." Cas rolled over until he was crouched above her, and their gazes locked.

"Sharing the flat implies a harmless bit of adults cohabiting." She looked away.

He wasn't sure what she was asking, or saying.

She'd told him she was unavailable. That this was a fling. Even as he'd accepted her terms, he'd known it wasn't a fling for him, but he'd been selfish enough to steal these weeks for himself.

It wasn't enough anymore.

"I'll wait for the questions, but Hunt's known me since I was a kid. Says he can read me like a book." He rubbed his nose against hers.

"He'll hardly ask if you're jumping my bones."

"He's more delicate in his questioning, but if he asks me if we're having a relationship I'll tell him the truth. He and

I have a rhythm, so I'll tell him." He smiled. "I don't regret a moment of the last month. Maybe making you spill your hot chocolate that first evening, but that's all. Will you tell Anna?"

"Girls do it differently," she said.

"You don't waste time on small talk. Straight into the details."

"I asked her to rate Hunter's kisses."

"What's my rating?" He nuzzled her throat.

"Good." She paused. "Heading toward great. Maybe stupendous. Can we talk about this tomorrow?"

Words to strike fear into a man's heart.

He rolled to the side of the bed. "There's not much point in pretending we're casual acquaintances at tonight's function after we shared our café kiss."

Her insistence on this niggled as well. Cas didn't plan to spend the night in her pocket. That wasn't their style, but he didn't want to pretend nothing had changed between them either.

"This is still a professional gathering."

"What? And we're not allowed to arrive together? What's your problem, Beatriz?" Unless he was the only one with skin in the game, and she hadn't changed her mind since they'd started this?

"Jackson Smithers is going to be there." She was rumpled from lovemaking, draped in a barely-there sheet and frowning.

"And? You'll have to do better than that."

"Martin was due to interview my intern Rachel this afternoon to ask about my backpack and whether anyone other than me touched it. Evidence to ensure that I won't be working as Jackson's personal lapdog."

"You think Jackson will come gunning for you at the function?" Cas hadn't considered that, and it explained some of Bea's off mood. "He'd be mad to do it."

"I don't know. I'm trying to minimise damage." She pushed off her side of the bed. "I'd better shower."

"We could shower?" He waggled his eyebrows, but she didn't bite. She was seriously rattled. "We play it your way." *To start.* "But, I'll drive us to the function. I'll drop you a block away and sort out a park. We can decide how we're getting home later."

"Thank you."

It took longer than anticipated for Cas to find a parking spot, so it was close to twenty minutes before he walked into the ballroom of the luxury hotel atop the city's remodelled historic sandstone post office—a ballroom now converted to an opulent conference venue. Cas stood near the entrance to survey the crowd. He knew about half the people present. Colleagues in his own and other companies, a number of existing clients, but it was his job to chat up the newcomers.

Forty minutes later, he was still circling. No one had asked him to his face if he and Beatriz were an item, but he'd seen a few glances slide from him to her, watched whispered conversations behind hands, a knowing smile exchanged. *Al'ama.* He'd kept his distance, behaved as he always did at these functions. She'd done the same.

He shouldn't have shared their first kiss in the café. It had shifted her work dynamic, and prompted gossip neither of them was comfortable with. Especially not his very private Ms. Gomez.

A spur-of-the-moment decision on his part, prompted by her nervousness, her bewilderment at her boss's betrayal, and his sudden lightbulb realisation that he'd always wanted to. He wasn't sorry, because it had given them a new starting point. He wanted to kiss her now, to draw her close and whisper in her ear that none of the gossip mattered. What mattered was what they were starting to create.

Except she insists we're just friends.

This, whatever we're doing that ends this weekend, is a fling.

"Hey, Cas."

Cas turned to shake the outstretched hand of the man approaching him, relieved to find a friend in the crowd. "I didn't expect to see you here, Antonio?"

"I've taken on Anna's load." Antonio grimaced.

"But you'd rather be elsewhere."

"The way you're looking at Beatriz, you'd rather be elsewhere."

Cas pushed a hand through his hair. "Am I that obvious?"

"Only to someone in a similar position, and you share some facial expressions with your sister."

"I'll take that as a compliment."

"Don't look now, but Jackson Smithers just arrived."

"Do you have a problem with him?" Cas glanced over his shoulder.

Jackson Smithers stood at the entrance, a woman on his arm. Young, obviously adoring. Instinctively, Cas searched the room for Beatriz. She looked stunned, as if someone had upended a bucket of icy water over her head. The intern. Jackson had got to Beatriz's intern.

"Al'ama." *The way things are going, I'll be needing stronger curses.*

"Anna warned me to be careful around him. Said he's a snake, and I trust her judgement. Antonio put a restraining hand on his arm. "You can't make a scene."

"He's about to."

Beatriz turned to the person beside her, her smile back in place, but the serpent had entered the garden.

"Speaking from experience, these functions aren't the place for Sir Galahad theatrics. Bea needs to handle this her own way."

* * *

Beatriz caught the heavily floral scent first, then the young woman came to a halt beside her.

"Can I steal Beatriz for just a minute," the young woman

said.

"Of course." The graphic artist who'd been asking Bea for the lowdown on Anna's honeymoon floated away.

"I didn't expect to see you here, Rachel?" Bea made it a question.

"Jackson brought me." She pointed toward where Jackson stood, leaning against a post, sending his minion to do his dirty work. Although Rachel probably didn't see it that way.

"It's good to have a guide to these functions. Your first few can be a bit intimidating." Bea forced herself to remain calm, but her stomach was churning at racing-yacht speed.

"Jackson told me what you were trying to do," Rachel said softly, her blood-red nails pressing against Bea's wrist, effectively holding Bea in place. "That you're jealous of him and told Martin he cheated at the interview. Said Jackson took something from your backpack."

"I'm not jealous." Bea looked her in the eye. "I'm angry."

"Same thing. I was interviewed. I told the truth. You asked Jackson to take the Landgemacht brochures from your backpack."

"You didn't hear me say that, because it's not true."

"Jackson told me you did. It's your word against his."

"It looks like it's my word against yours and Jackson's. You lied for him." The job she'd thought was safe wavered in front of her. Her small act of rebellion, which had seemed the perfect solution while sitting in Cas's arms, was a wet lettuce to Jackson's knife in the back.

"He earned that promotion." Rachel had taken a step back. *Good.*

"How?"

"He has the best ideas." Rachel looked across the room to Jackson for support.

"I'm guessing he told you that because the rest of us have been waiting for him to share a fresh idea since he arrived. If that's all you've come to say, you can go back to him now."

I will not call him your master, although he damn well is.

"Mission accomplished." Bea smiled and raised a hand in greeting to Jackson. The bastard.

"You'll be reporting to him now." Rachel spoke with such conviction, Bea's knees threatened to buckle.

I have to get out of here. No, I have to stay. If I run, Jackson will know he's won.

She searched the room, her gaze dancing over Cas. No, she wouldn't make him Jackson's next target.

Antonio was halfway down the room. Slowly, she made her way toward him, her heart beating frantically. She'd have to leave TBR. She'd go mad working for Jackson.

I can't leave until I find an equivalent salary package.

I don't care.

"Beatriz, let me take you home." Casildo appeared in front of her.

"No," she hissed. "Everyone will know."

Casildo's face went blank, but she read the hurt confusion in his eyes.

"Not about us." She waved a hand in the air, willing him to understand. "About Jackson."

When he continued to block her path, tears welled in her eyes. "Rachel lied for him."

"Where are you going?"

"Antonio. You shouldn't be near me."

Casildo turned on his heel and walked away. Bea took a step to call him back, then looked around. A few people were staring at her. She would not put Casildo in Jackson's gunsights, just when his dreams were within reach. Jackson had no scruples. He truly was the barbarian Casildo had identified.

And I can't stand in the middle of the room, looking as if I've seen a ghost.

She plastered a professional smile on her face and made her way toward Antonio. He kissed her cheek. She couldn't remember him ever kissing her cheek before.

"Tell me what you want me to do, Bea." Antonio's voice was low, steady, pitched so it wouldn't be heard by people nearby.

"Talk about work, about normal things." Bea hiccupped.

"Did Jackson threaten you?"

She stared at him, shock making her tremble slightly.

"Everyone gossips in our industry." His smile suggested they were sharing a joke. "You missed out on a promotion you deserved. Cas turned heads by kissing you in a coffee shop. I know Maha lent Cas her van a few weekends ago. Your turn to smile at me."

"I don't know what to say."

"Imagine you're wearing one of Anna's outlandish dresses."

Before meeting Hunter, Anna had occasionally used clothes to weed out the lechers from the good guys at industry functions.

"You want me to choose between her western bordello steampunk or her red sliced-to-the-navel *Killing Eve* dress? My mamá would have heart failure. I might have heart failure."

"I'm sorry I missed the western bordello. I gather there aren't even any photos of it."

"You'd have to ask Hunter." And Bea managed a small, genuine smile.

"Good woman. You're worried Jackson will go after Cas, aren't you?"

She nodded.

"Cas is tougher than he looks," Antonio said, drawing her toward the side of the room where friendlier colleagues welcomed her.

"But he's not a barbarian."

Antonio frowned, unaware of her meaning.

Bea had hurt Casildo, and she'd hurt him more before the night was out.

CHAPTER THIRTEEN

Rage and hurt battered at Cas, but beneath it, he was fighting confusion. He didn't know what had happened at the function, but it had scared Beatriz. No, terrified her, so time to suck up his rage until he understood why she'd turned her back on him.

Al'ama, it hurt. He couldn't remember being this afraid. Beatriz held his heart.

The key in the lock told him she'd arrived. He was ready. Calm, reasonable. She appeared in the doorway.

"What just happened, Beatriz?"

Okay, so I'm not calm or reasonable.

She turned her back on him. Ostensibly to shuck her coat, but it was another sting, another gut punch telling him something was wrong.

"And don't lie to me."

She swung back so fast, he was hit by the icy air she generated. "I've never lied to you."

"I'm sensing a but in there."

"We've both inserted buts in the last month."

"You said Rachel lied for Smithers. Does that mean she supported his version of the story to your boss?"

"She said I was jealous of his brilliance."

"Rachel's a naïve idiot. She lied, then she appeared at a function on his arm! How dumb does she think your boss is? If Martin can't see through that, then he deserves to lose you."

"Life's not that simple," she whispered.

"Stay?" Cas hadn't intended to start with this, but he could feel her retreating by the second. *I can't lose you.* He was scared. "Stay here with me?"

"Anna's going to rent the apartment." Her voice sounded far away.

"They know us. We wouldn't need references." Cas was racing toward a precipice ... he could see it in his head, but couldn't stop himself.

"You planned to live on your business premises. You can't afford the rent on this place."

"We could stay. We could share."

"I can't." Tears leaked from the corner of her eyes. "I'm sorry."

Cas flinched. "I thought we were in this together."

She reached out a hand to him, then pulled it back. "I can't afford to rent this apartment with you."

"You mean you don't want to." Despair dug its claws into him.

"I mean Jackson Smithers can do anything he likes." She dropped onto the sofa, rocking herself backward and forward. Shock?

"You're not making sense." Cas started to panic. Bent almost double on the sofa, she looked broken. Beatriz was strong. Why wasn't she fighting this? "Resign. Get another job."

"I can't."

"Why the hell not?"

"Because I can't afford to lose a single week's wages."

"You always make sense. You're not making sense now." Dread slithered through him. "Talk to me, Beatriz."

"The bulk of my wages goes directly to the bank to pay my parents' mortgage."

"Why?" He was struggling to connect the dots. Every week? All her money? And the weight of her dilemma cut through him.

"Because Papá's never fully recovered from his industrial accident. Mamá's worried half to death. They need to stop work, and they won't as long as they have a mortgage." She rushed her answer.

"They asked?" He'd met her parents. They wouldn't ask that.

"I offered," she whispered, dropping her head. "More than that. I promised."

"How long?"

"Two more years."

The gut punch was immediate. "That's a lot of money."

And explained all her unavailable vibes. Cas had given his father what must be a similar amount of money in a single hit. And his father had messaged that it would hit Cas's account by Monday.

"Why didn't you tell me?"

"Because it's my problem. My decision."

"Not fair, Beatriz."

"I told you I was unavailable. That this was a fling." But she breathed the words with a horror that revealed she was as aghast as he was.

"It stopped being a fling a long time ago."

Tears poured down her face. She didn't seem to realise she was crying. She loved him. He was sure of it. Every action, every touch, told him she loved him, but she'd made a promise to her parents. He knew what that was like.

"I thought this was a fling. A friends-with-benefits situationship while we stayed here."

She was digging a deeper hole with each word she uttered and didn't know it.

"Do that often?"

"No," she confessed, shame-faced.

"Right answer. But you assumed I did?" That stung. "Because of Monique?"

"No," she said. "But I was wrong."

"I told you about Nick Richardson's raid and why I needed free rent." He'd shared all his secrets. "Why not tell me then?"

"Because you also told me your father planned to give the money back. Now or never, you said." She reached a hand toward him and let it drop on her thigh. "We were talking about you achieving your dream. You're too good not to live that dream, and you need every cent you've saved to do it."

"What did you think would happen next week?" Cas demanded. "Just say goodbye. It's been nice. See you across a crowded room at the next cocktail function."

"I've tried not to think about it." She held up a hand. "Not true. I can't stop thinking about it. But I've tried to live in the moment."

"Doesn't ring true, Beatriz." He shoved his hands in his pockets, aware that at odd moments he'd wondered at the desperation in her lovemaking these last few days. "You do careful, detailed work. Everyone knows your planning skills are unbeatable."

"I took advantage of you," she whispered.

"You took advantage of *us*. I can't stay here. I need to think." He turned to leave, then swung back around. "One more question, why turn to Antonio tonight?"

"Antonio's untouchable. He owns his own business. He's had years in the business." Her face was pale, her eyes shadowed.

"You were protecting me from Smithers by letting everyone in that room know I didn't mean a damn thing to you? I'm secure in my job."

"You're about to start a new business," she snapped, seemingly goaded past breaking point.

"And you think I can't look after myself."

"It's a statement about his viciousness. Not a criticism of you." She looked like he felt. Blindsided by life.

"Thanks for the vote of confidence." He was gutted.

"I'm going out."

She nodded.

Somehow, he found himself at Hunter's. Sitting on the lounge where he'd shared beers, pizza, football games and deep and meaningfuls about life. Cas let the memories come. Beatriz had encouraged his dream, she'd found Mo. Although Mo would have approached him eventually. Or he hoped so. Beatriz made it happen sooner. She'd asked the probing questions, pushed him forward, all the time knowing that his father was about to give him back the money Cas had lent him. Savings that would set her free. Probably knowing she only had to ask.

She hadn't.

Cas started working backwards, examining the order of kisses, shared confidences, making love.

"A fling, Casildo. That's what we agreed."

It was never a fling for me. That's why I went slowly. I love you.

* * *

Bea closed her eyes. Why had she ever thought she should keep this from him. Why hadn't she anticipated this?

Because she hadn't dared think they had a chance beyond this month, hadn't dared to believe he could want more from her than a fling, that he might love her. Because she didn't want him to see her as another potential burden, as a gold digger, like Monique. Because she'd never stopped him when he'd talked about his family's assets.

"Where are you, Casildo?"

"The bulk of my wages go directly to the bank to pay my parents' mortgage."

She'd whispered the words while trying to make herself invisible, bewildered by how they'd started the evening with lovemaking and ended up in this conversation.

She'd been thinking non-stop about how to tell him

since they'd taken each other to bed the first time.

I didn't plan to tell you this way.

I love you.

I stop thinking when I'm with you.

I don't know how you feel about me.

But he'd asked her to stay.

She grabbed a pillow and, pressing it to her face, screamed into it, until she was hoarse.

I love you.

Enough to wish I'd never made the promise to my parents, to fantasise about the good fairy of the lottery, or the demon of the deep to magically transfer ginormous sums of money into my bank account. But her life wasn't like that.

She was crying, huge gulping sobs that stole her breath, and she couldn't make them stop.

This isn't me. I don't throw tantrums.

She stomped her feet. That was her before Casildo. Losing him was a physical ache, making her limbs heavy, her movements slow. She forced herself to shower, her tears carried away by the running water, brushed her teeth and screamed—silently this time—finally dressing in old jeans and one of Casildo's sweatshirts.

I'm only half-whole without you.

"Do something," she chastised herself, but she didn't know the woman she was berating. A woman who cursed her family, her history, her failure to see that she might have other better options if she abandoned her parents to manage by themselves.

As my sisters have. No, no, no.

She made herself do an inventory of supplies in the apartment, then took the list to the all-night supermarket and bought replacements for those staples she and Casildo had used. Not many. Neither of them had wanted to trespass on Anna and Hunter's generosity beyond the obvious gift of free rent.

Didn't that tell him anything about her?

Bea had only taken him home to meet her father and sisters the once.

Because she worried they might guess she was in love.

Because she'd built in the end of the relationship before she began. Casildo wouldn't see her as batshit crazy for helping her parents, but he wouldn't see her as honest either.

Back at the apartment, she busied herself making a simple pasta and a complicated chocolate dessert, and only realised she was crying again when tears rolled off her chin and onto the benchtop.

He didn't come home. He texted her around nine-thirty, saying that he'd dropped in to check Hunter's place and had decided to stay.

I understand: she'd texted back.

But Bea wasn't sure she did understand. He'd done almost exactly the same thing for his parents. Admittedly, he always had a promise of getting the money back, whereas she never would.

Had he stopped talking to her? She'd hurt him, implied he was a convenient screw, when she couldn't imagine her life without him.

And she couldn't tell anyone she was hurting too.

Got time for coffee?

Bea's finger hovered above *Send* on her phone. Anna had been back in Australia twenty-four hours. Allowing for jetlag and welcomes from immediate family, Anna was scheduled to start work today, so should have re-joined her everyday world by now. Bea gnawed her bottom lip. "Don't be such a wimp." She pressed *Send*.

Love to.

Bea stared at the phone.

Usual place for lunch?

Great, Bea replied.

That left her two hours and twenty-five minutes to get

her story straight for her friend. She wanted to ask for more time to spend with Casildo, but that was unfair to Anna. Basically unfair to her and Casildo as well. They needed to face reality, not bounce along in their own dream world as if happily-ever-afters were their right. But Bea wanted a few more days, so she could mend what she'd broken between them.

If Casildo let her.

He'd collected almost all his gear and gone while she was out.

Bea arrived at the small café midway between her office and Anna's early enough to snag a table in a quiet corner. She collected her Greek salad and some water from the fridge, then tried to organise her thoughts while she waited for her friend.

Anna breezed in ten minutes later, looking more relaxed and happier than Bea could ever remember seeing her. She came by the table before ordering food. Bea rose and hugged her. "Welcome back. You look happy."

"I don't remember ever being this happy. Marriage to Hunter is sexy, decadent, loving bliss." She squeezed Bea a little tighter. "And then some. Let me get something to eat and you can fill me in on all the gossip I've missed."

Bea knew Casildo would have messaged Hunter since the honeymoon couple had arrived back in Australia. She didn't know what he'd said, but Anna was her friend, so she needed to explain.

"You chose a salad?" Bea was momentarily distracted.

"I told you I was happy." Anna laughed.

"Did you have a taste bypass in Acapulco? I mean, you just don't eat salads as a rule."

"Weren't in Acapulco." Anna waved her fork in the air. "What have I missed?"

"I moved into your apartment the weekend you left."

"That's wonderful.

"Casildo did too."

"You moved in together?" Anna flopped back in her

chair. "I didn't see that coming. At least, I don't think I saw that coming. Should I have seen that coming?"

"It wasn't like that." Bea pushed her salad away.

"Like what?"

"Jackson Smithers got the promotion—"

"What!"

"He plagiarised my stuff." Bea waved a hand, dismissing Jackson Smithers to the irrelevance he deserved. "But I was upset. Turns out, my sisters were more upset about the loss of my pay increase, which they had plans for. I walked out."

"Bea, I'm so sorry. You earned that promotion."

"Don't get me started on justice in our industry. The point is I went to your place for time out. Maybe a few hours."

"And Casildo was already there."

"No."

"You asked him over?"

"I was curled up in the corner of the sofa, drinking hot chocolate, eyes shut while I listened to Taylor Swift set the world to rights. My idea of staying a few hours had morphed into a few days."

"Then you asked him over?"

"He arrived." Bea frowned, remembering the moment he'd called her name. Shock had shot her to her feet. She'd been wet and worried. "Maha said she wanted her granny flat back."

"Because"—the gears in Anna's brain visibly turned— "things have progressed far enough with Antonio that they wanted a bit of personal space."

"I didn't even know Antonio and Maha were an item."

"I know him." Anna shrugged. She'd worked for Antonio for years. "He looked a bit smitten at our wedding and surprised to be smitten. I can't recall him ever being seriously interested in a woman since his wife died. Maybe I'm wrong."

"You're not wrong. Casildo said he didn't ask his sister about her sex life."

Anna guffawed. "How's yours?"

Bea stared at her lunch.

"I'm sorry. I should know better than anyone not to ask personal questions."

"I gave him a week's trial," Bea said. "Said we could see if we got along as flatmates, but I was there first, and we both refused your offers to look after the apartment."

"I'm guessing you're getting along?"

"We were." Bea sipped her water.

"What do you want to tell me?" Anna touched Bea's hand.

Bea raised her head. "He's housetrained. He's thoughtful. We're lovers." She stumbled to a halt.

"What do you want to ask me?"

Coming between the new husband and wife had been another worry, so the gentleness in Anna's voice almost undid her. No shock, no recriminations, no "*Shit, you're talking about Hunter's best friend here.*"

Bea had thought long and hard about this. She was selfish, not wanting her time with Casildo to end, but she'd convinced herself Anna couldn't get the apartment rented out in a week. "Can I stay until next weekend, please?"

"You can stay as long as you want."

"That's not fair," Bea whispered. "To anyone."

"Are your parents financially dependent on you?" Anna was the only person who knew some of the truth.

"I'm paying most of the mortgage." A sob escaped. "They need to retire."

"How much longer?"

"Two years. A bit less." Bea had started counting the weeks, and that was insane.

"Do your parents know you've fallen in love?"

Bea flinched.

"You have, haven't you?" Anna's head was bent toward hers, her words impossible to hear if anyone was eavesdropping.

"They have to stop work, Anna. Papá particularly. He's

nearly a decade older than Mamá. The accident aged him even more. And I promised."

"You promised before you met Casildo."

"I had a crush on Casildo when we first met five years ago. I told myself it was a fantasy. Why would he ever look in my direction?"

"Because you're a lovely human being, and I'm guessing it's harder to tell yourself he's not interested now you've shared an apartment and his bed. Talk to your parents."

"I plan to talk to my parents. I won't bankroll my younger sisters anymore. It's time they got jobs and helped support themselves."

"That's a blessing."

"I thought you liked my younger sisters?"

"I do, but I love you, Bea. And they're far too comfortable with the tradition that the oldest daughter in a family is responsible for caring for her parents in their old age." Anna paused for a moment. "And you're not fighting me on this. Hallelujah."

"I've found myself wishing that I hadn't made such a big promise." The guilt accompanying those thoughts had almost paralysed her.

"What's Casildo think?"

"I'm not sure. Worried that I kept it a secret until now. Maybe deep down worried that I'm only interested in him because he comes from money."

"He wouldn't be so stupid."

"Casildo isn't stupid. He's hurt, but in his heart, he believes that promises to family are sacrosanct. He's struggling with what to believe."

"You're both idiots. Wonderful idiots."

"He's making some changes in his life too. He's committed to establishing his textile design business."

"Committed?" Anna hesitated, "That sounds like contracts signed and money committed."

"He's been sounding people out, waiting for the money to hit his account before he signs. It's due to hit his account this week."

"You're worried he might not go ahead?" Anna did that. Studied you with quiet intensity so you thought she could read your mind.

Casildo nourished Bea's soul, inflamed her body, sparked her imagination, and made her simply want to be with him. She yearned for him, and his words haunted her. She'd finally found someone she couldn't bear to live without.

"I said I wanted a time-limited affair because if he's to have a chance at his dream, he doesn't need another liability." Bea kept telling herself that. It was the truth, but her body and mind kept wanting to shut down each time she recited the words. "I'm also worried Casildo might throw in his lot with his father."

"Hunter hasn't mentioned anything."

"Has Hunter spoken to Casildo yet?"

"Not that I'm aware of. But Hunter's as focused on the Hariris's wellbeing as he is on his own."

Bea traced patterns on the tablecloth with the unused fork. "Casildo told me about Nick Richardson and what he tried to do. Is Hunter okay now? Are you okay?"

"Living and loving are works in progress, Bea. But we're focused on the future. Cas sounds like he's told you a hell of a lot?"

Bea nodded. "Casildo thinks he's failed his dad. Somehow it's tangled up with what happened with Monique?"

"Who's Monique?" Anna looked completely confused.

"Sorry. She's an old girlfriend of Casildo's who claimed she was carrying his child. She was lying, but they got as far as getting engaged, and he introduced her to the family, explained the situation."

"I didn't know. I love Hunter for a lot of reasons, but a biggie is that he never betrays confidences."

"She's not really important now"—Bea waved her fork in the air—"except?" She set the utensil down and frowned at the table. "Casildo has wanted to establish this business since he was a kid. It's a labour of love, but he also wants to make his father proud. He thinks he upset his parents with the Monique disaster. Now, I've hurt him. I'm worried he'll do something he'll regret later."

"I don't know him well enough to answer."

"Can you ask Hunter to make sure Casildo goes ahead?" Bea sounded pathetic to her own ears, and tears were threatening again. "I couldn't bear it if he didn't."

"A fortnight, Bea. Let me give you a fortnight?" Anna's concern was evident in her watchful eyes.

"You had a real estate agent lined up before you went away."

But Bea's resolve was wavering. Two weeks would give her time to talk to her parents and sisters, then leave them to come to terms with the changed situation before she moved home. Easier for her. *Who am I kidding?*

"They can wait."

"I'm not sure Casildo's talking to me at the moment. I want us to make peace before we go our separate ways."

I'd walk across broken glass for Casildo to tell me he understands. That he doesn't hate me.

"Did you go to work today?" Anna studied her closely.

"No." She pushed her salad around her plate.

"Something else happened. Can you tell me?"

"I told my boss Jackson Smithers stole my ideas. I said my intern Rachel could vouch for the fact he copied my project notes. She was interviewed on Friday. She said I lied because I was jealous of Jackson."

"Oh, honey." Anna reached across the table and squeezed her hand.

"Rachel shared this with me at the Faraday Cocktail Party on Friday evening. The idiot arrived with Jackson, spilled her poison with him looking on, then scurried back to him."

"Was Cas there?"

"That's what led to our bustup. He saw it, came to help,

and I brushed him off, didn't want Jackson to turn his guns on him."

"Cas is just as protective of those he loves as you are, Bea."

"If I keep my job after Rachel says I've lied, Jackson will probably get what he wants. He's decided I'll be working in a two-person team with him on innovative ideas." She lifted her head to meet Anna's gaze. "I am so angry, I could choke. But I need the job, and I need Jackson to stay away from Casildo." The tears she'd fought to keep at bay fell as fast as she blotted them away.

"We'll fight." Anna moved to sit beside her, both facing the back wall.

Bea gave a watery chuckle, leaning her head on Anna's shoulder. "I feel like I've been fighting for years."

CHAPTER FOURTEEN

Cas had stayed in Hunt's spare bedroom the first night. Maybe he should have moved in there in the first place, but the idea of somewhere different, then the idea of sharing with Beatriz had taken hold. Now, he was rattling around the empty, lonely house attached to Niall Quinn's workshop.

Hell. Bloody perishing hell.

Beatriz had said that when she'd upended his box of books on their first Saturday together. The first time she'd challenged him about his plans.

"I've seen your wedding gift to Anna and Hunter."

She called him to meet Mo.

She talked graphic design software.

She tossed around ideas, made him laugh and then made glorious love to him.

He punched the pillow and rolled over.

I sleep better with her beside me. When did that happen?

He flopped to his other side.

What they shared was so far beyond the sex he'd had with other women. She'd pushed aside all his barricades with her laughter and passion. Passion for *him*. She made him feel special, lavishing attention on his body, but also whispering words of encouragement, of pleasure and happiness, and she fed his confidence until he believed he could achieve his dreams out of bed.

She'd made a promise to her parents. Promises were sacrosanct in his family.

Needing to get his thoughts straight, he headed back to Anna's apartment before dawn, brewed Beatriz's must-have ginger tea, knocked on her door and pushed it wide. The bedclothes were a tangled mess around her feet. Instead of her usual nakedness—another little spurt of rebellion she'd gloried in—she was wearing one of his shirts.

Tousled, bleary-eyed, and he'd give her every cent he had if she asked him to and to hell with the consequences. He sat on the side of the bed while she wriggled backward until her back was against the headboard. Her toenails were purple and yellow this week. Irrelevant, but maybe sharing his bed had been another act of rebellion. Not his money, but bragging rights about his body.

She's not like that.

"I've got your tea." He handed her the cup.

She wrapped her hands around it, took her first sip and closed her eyes.

"First sip. Every day, and you get this ecstatic expression on your face."

"Sorry." She lowered the cup.

"What for?"

"For disappointing you. For not telling you sooner that I'm not in a position to share anything with anyone."

"I'm not anyone, Beatriz." Or so he'd hoped.

"No, you're not. And I owe you an apology. I've loved sharing with you, living with you, making love to you, I"— she was unsmiling and had shadows in her eyes—"but I have to go home."

"That simple?" Had she been going to say she loved him? Fool that he was, he wanted to hear those words from her.

She winced. "It's not simple, and it's not easy, but it's my only current, viable option."

He'd told himself the same thing after he'd handed his father his savings. He'd gone home.

Do you love me?

He wasn't brave enough to ask, but he couldn't sleep, couldn't eat, and sure as hell couldn't see his life anymore without her in it.

"What about now?" he said.

"I don't want us to part in anger, Casildo. You said we'd always be friends." She sounded wistful, and sad with it.

"You might not get all you want."

He couldn't stay and not touch her. He'd come to confirm that truth. He loved her, and he believed her.

"Why didn't you tell me at the beginning?" It seemed so out of character for the Beatriz he knew. Not a direct lie, but a consequential omission that was hurting them both.

"I don't tell anyone," she cried. "I was dating someone—we'd got a bit past dating—when Papá had his accident. Fernando resented the time I spent at the hospital. I was supposed to put his needs, his demands, his requirements—he used that word—before everyone else. He insisted I was his woman."

"He didn't know you."

"He'd acted a bit strangely when another guy chatted to me at a party. I didn't take him seriously. More fool me."

"He was the idiot," Cas said, hurt anew by the realisation Beatriz didn't have a mean or avaricious bone in her body. He loved her, and she was leaving him.

"But jealous of my family? Papá? Papá nearly died." She hiccupped. "I haven't dated anyone since. Mamá and Papá need to stop work."

"Are you asking me for money?" Cas forced the words out.

She recoiled, her shoulders arching, her body contorting in pain. "No, I'm not bloody asking you for money."

"You were waiting until I'd got the contracts lined up and the money in the bank before telling me, weren't you?

Why?" The contracts were sitting unsigned on his desk.

She looked like a floodlit hibernating bear, simultaneously irritated and disoriented. "Because you've waited years for your dream, Casildo. Your time's now."

"You know I can't stay here."

Tears leaked from the corners of her eyes. She made no attempt to brush them away. "I understand."

He left before he took the words back, before he touched her. If he touched her, he'd crawl beneath the sheets and make love to her as he had every morning for the past fortnight. He loved her, but that meant nothing unless he could solve her problems and seize his dream.

* * *

Bea dragged herself around the apartment after Casildo left, unable to sleep, to concentrate, unable even to decide whether to get dressed or not. When the phone signalled an incoming message, she lunged for it, then stifled a sob when it wasn't Casildo.

She blinked, then stared at the text. A summons to meet her boss. One day she'd taken off, but she hadn't taken a day off in five years without giving advance warning. Was she about to lose her job as well as lose Casildo? Get sacked for making false complaints about Jackson? Great.

At least Martin had scheduled the meeting for eight o'clock. Before the bulk of the staff arrived. She might be in and out before anyone knew.

She applied more makeup than usual. No one needed to know that she'd spent the last few days crying. For Casildo. Jackson was a lying cheat and would be caught out sooner or later. He wasn't worth her tears. She slipped in through the back entrance, studied the lobby until she knew she'd be alone in the elevator. The corridor leading to Martin's office was oddly quiet—and endless. Sucking in a deep breath, she exhaled and knocked on the door.

"Come in, Beatriz." Martin pulled his door wide.

Spotting the other people in the room, Bea stopped dead.

"Jackson and Emily Carlsson are joining us as well. You know Jackson, but I don't believe either of you have met Emily. Emily, perhaps you can introduce yourself."

"*Hej.* I'm the cyber tracker TBR has started using to improve data protection." The woman sounded Swedish.

Bea was confused, but with her life completely upended, what did one more mystery count?

"There have been a spate of ransomware attacks in the industry recently," Martin said smoothly, "and we have so much confidential client information in our files that we decided to upgrade all our systems."

"I didn't know that," said Jackson.

"It's not news we wanted to broadcast," said Martin. "But it's a necessary business precaution these days."

"Cyber security," Bea whispered. She'd given permission for all her work files to be remotely accessed and searched when she'd lodged her complaint about Jackson.

"But ransomware isn't the reason I called this meeting." Martin looked at her. "Unfortunately, I had to be away from the office late last week, so missed some key staff meetings. I understand a few decisions were made that will need to be reversed. I wasn't present for Rachel Wallace's interview on Friday, but I've read the transcript."

Jackson shifted in his seat.

"Jackson, did Beatriz give you permission to go through her backpack and copy her notes on the Landgemacht project?"

Bea lifted her gaze to Jackson's face. It was one thing to get Rachel to lie for him, a different thing for him to lie. Her hand crept to her throat. What files had the super-efficient Emily Carlsson been delving into? She could see Jackson making swift calculations, assessing what he'd get away with.

"I might have misunderstood her, but we've been working together on a few things, and she's given me permission to share." Jackson threaded a hand through his hair, disarranging it in a way that had Rachel drooling, then gave one of his boyishly charming smiles, that always left Bea's teeth on edge.

"Not those files," Bea disagreed. Martin had listened to her when she'd asked to speak to him about the interview after her pep talk with Casildo.

Bea had suggested a cyber security system as a line item for Casildo's business plan to prevent hacking of his accounts, or theft of his designs. She hoped he'd follow up. Maybe Anna could get Hunter to drop a hint.

"The search and data evidence support Beatriz's statement to me that she privately developed some ideas to present as part of her promotion interview," Martin said. "The files were locked, but a single copy was printed. You quoted extensively from that file in your interview and claimed the ideas were yours."

"We must have talked about them, thrown ideas back and forth," Jackson pushed ahead, claiming credit when his cover was blown.

"You requested that Beatriz work exclusively for you on Friday."

"We're a good team."

"Never gonna happen," Martin said. Not an expression she could recall her boss ever using before. "Collaboration is one thing. Theft is another. And intimidation of another employee is a sackable offence."

"If Beatriz said I intimidated her, that's a lie." Jackson did outrage very well.

"The principal of a rival firm made an official complaint to me yesterday."

Antonio? Casildo wasn't a principal of any firm. Yet.

"Did you put your boyfriend up to this?" Jackson sneered.

Jackson had taken the bait, turned his attention to Antonio, not Casildo. Casildo was safe. Relief made her dizzy.

"There's no evidence that Ms. Gomez and Mr. Perez

have a personal relationship, however, there is evidence that you contacted the independent on the interview panel prior to the interview," Emily was clinical in her conclusion.

Bea could get addicted to Emily's Swedish accent.

"I'd like your resignation, effective immediately, Jackson." Martin stood and opened the door.

"I can explain," Jackson started.

"I'd also like you off the premises in fifteen minutes. Emily will assist you to clear your desk."

Bea watched Emily and Jackson leave in a kind of fog. What had just happened? And why couldn't it have happened last week before Rachel and Jackson ambushed her?

"I'm sorry, Bea. My son copped a cricket ball to the head last Wednesday. I've been at the hospital."

"Is he okay?"

"He'll be fine." Martin exhaled slowly. "I intended to take Emily with me to Rachel's interview on Friday. But nothing went according to plan. Do you want some time off?"

"Yes, please," she managed. *I have to tell Casildo.*

"I don't blame you. Antonio raked me over the coals for the disrespect shown to you. Said he was of a mind to offer you a job himself. I hope you don't accept, but I wouldn't blame you if you did. We let you down."

"Antonio hasn't spoken to me."

"The promotion's yours, if you want it."

"I appreciate the offer. Thank you. I need some time."

If I accept, I can pay the increase in the mortgage. The relief was dizzying.

"Maybe you can call me on Friday and give me your decision?"

Beatriz couldn't remember how she made it back to the apartment or the kitchen. She glanced at the oven clock. Midday.

How long have I been here?

Her body ached, her muscles screaming with the effort

of responding to simple commands, like walk, undress, crawl into bed. She'd barely slept since Casildo had left. Missing him was the largest part, but waiting for Jackson's next hit, to her or Casildo, had also kept her awake.

My boss was absent on Friday. Family emergency. Jackson's lies uncovered. Antonio lodged formal complaint about Jackson. Jackson sacked. Effective immediately.

She pressed *Send* and headed for the bedroom.

I'm happy for you.

Casildo's reply was fast, generous, but left no openings. Bea was crying when she climbed under the covers.

CHAPTER FIFTEEN

Cas typed a text, then shook his head. *Déjà vu.*

Over the years, he'd sought Hunt out too many times to count. Cas hadn't always been the one in trouble. Best friend, blood brother, so he'd ask to see Hunt privately if he had to. Hunt could decide how much he'd tell Anna. Probably everything.

I love Beatriz.

Safe was the word that came to mind. He'd known he was safe with Beatriz before they made love, but the emotional intimacy that came from sharing a bed, from sharing thoughts and dreams and silly jokes with a lover like Beatriz gave safety a depth and joy he'd never experienced before. He couldn't lose it.

I never told her I love her.

Time to let his blood brother know he'd arrived. Cas pressed *Send* on the text.

Hunt opened the door, then with a huge grin dragged him into a bearhug. "I missed you."

"Me too." A month was probably the longest Cas hadn't seen Hunt since they were kids.

"Come on up?" Hunter took the stairs at a trot, his contentment tangible.

"Is Anna here?"

"She's over at Liam and Kate's; she's been missing her new niece."

"Are you and she thinking of making your own baby Lily?" Adulthood kicked you in the balls sometimes. Life changed when you married, when you found someone you wanted permanently in your life. Like Beatriz.

"Not just yet. We want some time living together first." Hunter crossed the living area toward the kitchen. "We did things arse around—married, now we're living together. Anyway, I'll grab some beers. You might like to check out the bedroom first."

"Why would I check your bed—"

Hunter grinned.

Cas pushed the door wide. The bed was made up with the linen doona cover and pillowcases he'd designed and had made as a wedding present. The cushion covers had been filled and were stacked along the window seat.

Hunter passed him a beer. "They're fantastic, bro. Anna doesn't want to sleep under anything else."

"I'm glad." Cas sipped his beer.

"She asks me to tell her the stories behind some of those items you've hidden in the undergrowth, like our billy cart, or the tumbling dollars half buried in the dirt."

"Good bedtime stories." Cas toasted him with his bottle.

Hunter snorted. "Right." Then ambled back to the loungeroom. "Want pizza?"

"Is this a boys' night?" Cas's mood shifted. He'd been hoping for some alone time, but hadn't expected the newlyweds to want to part even for a few hours. Maybe he didn't need to unburden himself straight away. Maybe he could just hang, find his balance.

Except I don't have time.

"It is. And marriage doesn't mean they're at an end. Anna lectured me before she went out. It's important to maintain friendships and do some separate things occasionally."

"Sounds like you didn't spend a second apart on your honeymoon."

"I love her. She loves me. I can't find the words for how wonderful that is."

"In that case, pizza works."

Hunter made the call and gestured to the opposite sofa. "Let's get comfortable. How's life?"

"A few hiccups." Cas was too restless to sit.

"You don't have to tell me …"

"But I might feel better if I do." A patter he and Hunt had tossed at each since time began, or since they'd become blood brothers. Cas hid little from Hunter. "You know the situation I'm in better than most. Although you might not have had a chance to catch up yet. Dad's money has come through. He's transferred my share to me." Cas paused, then chose his words carefully. "But I've been wondering about Dad. His future isn't as settled as he'd expected it to be. As I'd expected it to be."

"Have you talked about your business plans with him?"

Hunter had leapt continents with that question.

"Not since my last year of high school when, after a tense conversation, which you mediated, Dad accepted that I'd do a business degree, with specialisation in marketing and graphic design."

"He was concerned. Making a living from art, any artistic endeavour, is hard. Think music, think performance, and textile design is a contested space."

"Are you sure he wasn't pushing for me to take over? Most of the skills in my business degree translate."

An old niggle, one Cas had thought he'd put to bed. But Beatriz's situation had him questioning everything, and joining the family business would free up his savings.

"I'd have said Raed Hariri's one of the most clear-sighted people I know. He might be questioning your commitment these days because you've achieved success in advertising. He *wonders* if you've abandoned textile design, and you leave him in ignorance."

Cas noted Hunt's emphasis on *wonders*.

"Maybe you should invite him up here and show him my bed linen." Cas opted for flippancy while he shifted arguments in his head.

"Maybe you should design some for him and your mum." Hunt watched him with the same intensity he'd watched him when they first met, deciding what lay behind the words, familiar with words not matching intentions. "If anyone is suited to take over, it's Maha. She hides her business genius behind her second love—childcare. She's also as bad as you at asking for help."

Cas never had, because his goals were so far from the family's natural trajectory.

"Maha was ready to open a second centre, desperate to help your dad, yet I had to ask if she'd like to move into The Hariri."

"I missed that."

Although he remembered the ease with which Maha had joined the business conversation, talking about costs and benefits, depreciation on capital, ongoing maintenance of the building, refurbishment, and so much more that Cas was only absorbing in his most recent studies.

"You had a lot going on. And you were worried about your dad and *me*. Business runs through her veins, like design runs through yours."

"You got both."

"What can I say? I'm a Renaissance man." Hunter was gently mocking him.

"But you've ended up at the business end of the scale. How do you feel about that?"

"I'm changing direction again," said Hunter. "More project management, matching the right people to the right projects."

"Maybe you should manage me?" Cas was only half-joking.

"Except we confront the Hariri family problem of struggling to ask for help. You've never asked for help for yourself, Cas." Hunter's phone sounded. "That'll be the pizza. I'll go down and get it."

Cas paced for the few minutes Hunter was gone. Better just to get it out there. He pivoted on his heels when he heard his friend re-enter the room.

"I'm considering putting my business plans on hold." Cas had drafted their eulogy.

"Why now? And sit, will you? You've got the funds you need."

"I should have seen it coming." Cas threw himself onto a sofa.

"What? The attack on your dad? I didn't." Hunt set the pizza box on the table and sank into the opposite sofa. "What makes you a better barometer for Nick Richardson's vicious plots than me?"

"I'd stopped paying attention. I only half-listened when Dad mentioned odd patterns, graffiti on buildings, petty vandalism, tenants saying questions hadn't been answered when Dad said he hadn't received any questions."

"You're claiming responsibility for Nick's sins now. Where the hell is this coming from, Cas?"

"It's not the money. Or not just being bested in business. Dad's in retreat. He hunkers in his office all day, but he won't talk to me."

"Do you want me to talk to him?"

"I'm a failure as a son." Cas bounced back to his feet and started pacing.

"That's pretty comprehensive. Why?"

"I've been talking of my own business for years, but never made the move."

"For a variety of reasons—very good reasons—you haven't been in a position to until now."

"Well, now I'm thinking about a change in direction. I've been doing research in your absence." Research for his own business, but hell, his life had been turned upside down by Beatriz's revelation. "You asked me to keep an eye on things in your absence. I've been paying attention."

"Remind me again why your parents moved to Australia?"

"Because Dad recognised after Maha's birth that his daughter or daughters wouldn't be able to live fully independent lives in Saudi Arabia."

"Did you listen to what you just said? Raed Hariri doesn't follow traditional expectations. He might occasionally fantasise about you following in his footsteps, more when you were a kid, but he worked out pretty quickly you'd be miserable."

"Then why the fight about my degree?" Cas had latched on to the memory in the last few days.

"Already answered that one. Because more people fail than succeed in the creative industries. He wanted you to have a backup plan. We beat this to death at the time, Cas."

"Maybe I should offer to join the business?"

"Why the fuck would you do an insane thing like that?" Hunt pushed the pizza box away from him. "And for fuck's sake, sit down. You're giving me neck ache."

"He's withdrawn. He sits in his office. For hours. That's not him." Cas pushed a hand through his hair, and returned to the sofa.

"That very definitely is him. All the Hariris are workaholics. Have you asked if anything is wrong?"

"No. I've been working on a plan. Something to put on the table."

"And part of that plan is to lose everything you've worked for?" Hunter was preternaturally calm, while Cas became more agitated.

"I've got very little."

"How many children do your parents have?"

"Is this a trick question?"

"Not from where I'm sitting."

His friend was outwardly cool as crisp lettuce, but Cas knew him better than almost anyone on earth.

"Dad always says four. If pushed, he says three biological and one adopted."

"What do *you* say in the quietness of the night when you're telling yourself you're a failure?" Hunter was moving his beer from one hand to the other.

"You're the son he should have had. You saved him, and I didn't." Cas leaned forward, his hands between his knees.

"When did it become a competition?" Hunter's eyes narrowed.

"Al'ama. You're my brother, Hunt. I'm sorry, I'm cocking this up too."

"'Cocking it up' is not a phrase I associate with Casildo Hariri. Eat some pizza, and tell me what the fuck is going on."

"You've been away, Hunt. Staying in the granny flat, I saw Dad every day. I can't see any other way to help him except to join the business."

Having his savings in reserve to help Beatriz would be the bonus.

"Have you considered he might refuse?"

"I do have that business degree, you know," Cas snarled, reaching for a slice of pizza.

"Raed Hariri's business is rock solid. Until Nick Richardson sabotaged the tenancies in the Sydney building, it was paying its way. Most of your father's assets are in regional NSW. Small holdings—shops and other commercial premises that deliver reliable returns. While those investments are gold-plated, regional properties generally take longer to sell than city properties."

"How come you know all this?"

"Because despite being his second son and your brother, I did due diligence. I couldn't afford to overcommit myself. Then we'd all have been cactus."

"Then explain his behaviour."

"I'm not convinced it's abnormal yet. I can guess that being threatened might make him reassess what's happening in his world, where he wants to be in five or ten years' time. Knowing his son was prepared to give up his own dream to help him would have shaken him. Parents are supposed to look after their children, remember? You told me that. I've certainly reassessed my life since meeting Anna. I don't want the same things. To be blunt, you sound like you've been reassessing as well."

"Beatriz says I've got more business acumen than I give myself credit for." Cas wasn't sure why he'd said that except it brought Beatriz into the conversation.

"Whoa. That's what this is about? Beatriz?"

"I could be useful to Dad."

"Beatriz said you could be useful to your dad?" Hunter scoffed his disbelief. "In what universe? You've been making connections in the textile printing world for years, making connections with distributors, testing out your designs at markets and small trade fairs. You could be far more useful to yourself."

Hunt wasn't letting him off the hook.

"Beatriz says I have the skills and experience to make a go of my own business." Cas sighed. Beatriz made him believe he could run his own business. He just wasn't sure he wanted to do it without her.

"Smart woman, Beatriz Gomez." For Hunter, that was a question. "Kind of cute too."

"You've got your own woman."

"Who's occasionally cute." Hunter grinned. "So, is Beatriz your woman?"

"Because it's you, I won't clock you for that sexist remark. Beatriz and I are—"

"You can't finish that sentence."

"You're not going to call me on messing with Anna's friend?"

"From what I've heard so far, neither of you is messing."

"She needs money." Cas deflated.

"Has Beatriz asked you for money?"

"Never." And she never would. Cas knew that, which made winning her back harder. "She can't move in with me, because she can't pay her share of costs."

"Sorry if I seem a bit dense here, but how did the topic

of Beatriz moving in with you come up? When we left for our honeymoon, you were in Jaddatee's flat."

"We're staying in Anna's apartment." Cas waved a hand in the air. "It started as a mix-up. Beatriz went there seeking refuge from her sisters. Maha asked for her granny flat back."

"It's got two bedrooms." Hunter's voice was bland. His eyes twinkled.

"Did Anna tell you?"

"Anna mentioned a mix-up. Said you'd reached a compromise to share—"

"Al'ama. Anna told you we're sharing a bed."

"Anna didn't use those words."

"Is that why Anna's out tonight?"

"Part of it. She said Bea asked her for another week. Anna got her to accept two."

"Two weeks won't make a difference except to drive me crazy. I've moved out."

"Where?"

"The house attached to Niall Quinn's workshop is empty since he and Lucy got together. I asked if I could stay for a few weeks."

"Why didn't you ask me?"

"For the love of all things holy, you're not going to have a snit, because I didn't ask you. You weren't even here."

"Anna said Bea wants to make peace."

"Beatriz has become a fantasist."

And his need to prove himself to his father and rescue Beatriz were tearing him in two.

Cas had lived comparatively happily within the boundaries he'd set for himself. Until Beatriz. Until Beatriz shared excitement and laughter and passion with him and told him about her promise to her parents. There was no way Beatriz saw his father's bank balance when she looked at him.

I'm thinking of giving Beatriz my money.

"That's where the idea for joining the family business

comes from?"

Cas should have expected Hunt to join the dots.

"Has your father ever offered you a job?"

"I made it clear I wasn't interested. It's different now." Cas clenched his jaw. "Beatriz is desperate to support her family. She promised."

"What did she promise?"

"To pay the bulk of the mortgage until it's paid off. I'm pretty positive she's helping her sisters too." He lowered his voice. "Her family comes before me."

And that was the hardest truth to confront. He was low on her list of priorities. If he'd even made it to the list.

"You think you don't matter to her?"

"Her sisters were angry she missed out on a promotion. Because they had plans for the money. That's why she fled to Anna's apartment. She glossed over their selfishness."

"You think she should have blurted out her life story to you when her family had just let her down?" Hunt never let him off the hook. "If you didn't matter, surely she'd have taken the money?"

"When you say it like that." Cas scowled.

"I'll give you something for nothing. Anna shared this and gave me permission to tell you. Bea has always paid board and helped her family out in tight times. She doesn't talk about it, because a guy she trusted with her secret ditched her, implying she wanted a sugar daddy."

"Yeah. She told me. And I have a history with gold diggers."

"You told her about Monique?"

"I tell her everything."

"Would you break a promise to me for her?" Hunt's quiet voice was sharper than a rapier.

"I might want to," Cas admitted, meeting his best friend, brother-in-all-except-blood's gaze.

"What if you'd had to choose between giving her or your dad your life savings?"

Cas flinched.

"Then I'm guessing you can see her dilemma. Does she know what you were saving for?"

"Yes."

"She didn't ask for your help. Sounds exactly like you, Cas. You don't ask."

"I've got a few plans I've been working on, not just joining the business."

"Tell me."

"I pay half of her mortgage payments. She pays half, then she's got enough to pay the rent, and I start my business more slowly than planned."

"This is your alternative to giving her your savings and going to work for your father, whether he wants you to or not." Hunter held Cas's gaze. "Why would she accept that?"

"Family—if we marry—"

"Whoa. I must have missed steps one through ninety-nine, the ones between sharing a bed and marriage. What about your vow after Monique?"

"Beatriz has exorcised Monique."

"How, because Maha and I sure the hell tried hard enough to." An edge of frustration had entered Hunt's usually calm voice.

"Beatriz wants me to succeed. Me, Casildo Hariri."

That's what he'd finally realised. Beatriz saw him, not his family's wealth, not his current job description. That's how he knew she loved him, even if she didn't know it yet.

"We all want you to succeed, you idiot, including Raed. Maybe Raed the most. I love your heart and your loyalty. I love that you're my brother, but giving up your dream isn't the answer." Hunt shifted to sit beside him.

"I might have a better plan."

"You'd better, because *if*—and your plan is riddled with ifs—if Beatriz accepts half your money, and if she agrees to marry you, you could lose the business and her anyway. She'll always feel guilty, wonder if you're doubting her love. That's a recipe for hell on steroids."

"I need your help." Cas had said the words, and the

world hadn't ended.

"Are those words really so hard to say?" Hunt stared straight ahead, a concession so he wasn't looking at Cas's face as Cas made the stupid confession.

"Plan A was kneejerk, although I have been worried about Dad. I don't want to follow in Dad's footsteps."

"We all know that."

"And given how many nights I badgered you with my ideas, you also know I fell in love with my granny's fabrics when I crawled over every surface in her flat as a baby. Slippery, knobbled, warm, cool, slinky, comforting—I learnt a whole vocabulary from her."

"I know you adored her. I'm sorry I only met her a few times." Hunter's voice was low, designed to keep him talking.

"Even more, I don't want to disappoint Dad anymore. The first time Dad took me to The Hariri building, him in his suit, me in short pants and my first jacket, I was about five or six. Dad was glowing as the sign-writers mounted the sign. One of them patted my head. 'Not long before you'll be handing over to this one,' he said. The lawyers were inside. 'Brought your son along to see his inheritance.'"

"Do you ever think Raed might have had something to prove to his dad? He left his home, his family, his religion to give his daughters opportunities. That would have been tough. You're very like him. I'm guessing that's why you've been so determined to establish your business without help."

"I *have* felt guilty that I've disappointed him. Never asking for help to achieve my dreams was my cack-handed apology for not wanting what he wanted."

"Very like him." Hunt nudged his shoulder.

"My stuff up with Monique disappointed him," Cas confessed his deeper worry.

"That's not my reading of the situation. You should ask him."

"I'll be asking him a lot of things. I can't lose Beatriz."

"What can I do?"

"Will you be my business partner, Hunt? I know you refused Dad, but I'm asking you to be my partner in this."

"You want me to draft the clauses so you're not responsible for any losses?"

"You're a dickhead."

"Another un-Cas-like remark, although I reckon your jaddatee would grant you a little slack, considering the circumstances."

"I want to create enough space for me to pay the rent on an apartment, then ask Beatriz to share." He'd convince her to agree. "So, is that a yes?"

"Are you sure?"

"About you? I should have asked years ago. About Beatriz? I was sure before we made love, but making love to Beatriz is the most wonderful thing that ever happened to me. Does that make sense?"

"To me it does. Tell me what you need me to do. And talk to Raed."

"I will."

Then I need to convince Beatriz this will work.

CHAPTER SIXTEEN

Bea's mother was already seated when Bea arrived at the restaurant the Gomez family favoured for special occasions. Just the three of them tonight. Bea couldn't remember the last time she'd eaten in a restaurant with just her parents, if ever.

Butterflies, of the kind she'd only experienced a few times in her life, bounced around her belly. Trepidation, like the time she'd waited at the hospital for her middle sister's birth, when the doctors had said it was touch-and-go for mother and child, when her father had been injured at work, and her mother had taken off at a run, leaving Bea to explain and console her younger sisters. Terrors that hadn't become disasters.

Losing Casildo was a disaster on a scale of its own.

She understood her promises to her parents, understood Casildo's promise to himself. Understanding made no difference. His presence had become essential to her happiness, to her ability to breathe freely, to put one foot in front of the other, to string words together. She was a fool ever imagining a few weeks of Cas's lovemaking would be enough. She'd known it, but taken all she thought was on offer.

"Hola, Mamá." Bea bent to kiss her mother's cheek, before taking the second seat at the table set for three. "Where's Papá?"

"He'll be here soon. I wanted a few minutes to myself with you."

"Is something wrong?"

Bea checked her memory for something important she'd missed, some responsibility she'd forgotten because she couldn't think past abandoning Cas. Except he was the one who'd moved out. She was staying at Anna's the extra two weeks to get her emotions in check. She kept bursting into tears at the stupidest things—a bottle of beer in the fridge, a T-shirt Casildo had left behind. She should move back home.

Except she needed time alone to grieve.

"Who's the man?"

"There isn't a man." Denying Casildo made her heart break just that little bit more.

"*Claro que no*, but you had a glow, Beatriz. The same glow your sisters had when they introduced me and Papá to the boyfriends who became their husbands. And now you don't."

"He's a friend." Although she wasn't sure of that anymore.

"It's good to be friends with the man you love." Her mother took her hand under the table.

"Love isn't enough," Bea said. Despite all the hype and social media promises.

"Without love, you have nothing."

"I'm not without love." Bea let some of her frustration show. "You and Papá love me, on a good day, my sisters love me."

"It's not the same, and I hope you're not giving up this friend because of your family." Her mother's rebuke made her feel five years old. "Tell me his name."

"Casildo Hariri." Saying his name hurt.

"I guessed."

"Guessed what?"

"There's a photo of you smiling at each other in Anna and Hunter's wedding photos. He came to pick you up when you moved out. You brought him to dinner when I asked. Tell me about him."

"He's Hunter's best friend. His family's lovely. They adopted Hunter unofficially. There are two sisters, one married."

"You've met his family." Another rebuke.

"It's complicated, but Casildo asked me to go to dinner with him, his parents, his eldest sister and the man she's seeing. Sort of run interference for them."

"And you could run interference because you were a new couple?"

"He's Hunter's best friend and I'm Anna's. We were missing them. It was a friendly invitation, like yours."

"Tell me more about this friendly boy?" Her mother patted her leg under the table.

"He works in advertising, but his dream is to design and create beautiful textiles. For homes, not for fashion. He's been sharing Anna's apartment with me for the last month."

"Ah. I wondered who you were living with."

"It was an accident. We both needed a bolthole and turned up on the same day, so we agreed to share. It has two bedrooms."

"I'm sorry you needed a bolthole."

Bea winced.

"But it made us rethink some timelines on our plans," her mother said. Before Bea could ask what she meant, her mother continued, "I hope you didn't waste a whole month sleeping in separate bedrooms."

"Mamá!"

"You had that glow." Her mother's face became wreathed in smiles.

"That's what I want to talk to you about. Talk to you and Papá about."

The promotion would cover the increase in the

mortgage payments. As Casildo would say, *Thank you, Jaddatee.* Now, she was looking for extra work to pay her share of rent on an apartment with Casildo.

Then, I'll ask him to take me back.

"Here comes Papá." Her mother made the words an announcement, as if the sun, the moon and stars had stepped into the restaurant. She'd always been like that. Her parents had always been like that.

"How are my favourite girls?" Her father kissed her mother, then Bea.

"We're good. And ready for that champagne now," Mamá said.

"Are we celebrating something?" Bea croaked, struggling to stay focused. She'd just confessed to her very upright mother that she and Casildo had been living together.

"Me confessing that Papá and I anticipated our wedding vows by quite a few months. When we had enough money to rent a garage, we stopped taking precautions. Our families insisted on marriage when I said I was pregnant."

"They'd been against the idea until then," her papá added, "and we had no place to go. We had to get a room first." He signalled the waiter. "A bottle of your best champagne." He smiled at her mother. "I didn't know that's what we were celebrating."

"Beatriz has something to tell us. Her news might be better than ours."

The waiter returned, popped the cork and poured three flutes of champagne, before discreetly disappearing.

Bea looked from her mamá to her papá's faces. "Here goes. I'll continue to make payments on the mortgage, but only the mortgage." Her stomach was a mass of marauding elephants. She sucked in a breath and continued, "Lisa and Fran will have to start pulling their weight, maybe even get part-time jobs."

"Stop." Mamá passed Bea her flute. "Time for the first toast."

"To the independence of all our daughters." Papá waved his glass in her direction, seemingly indifferent to whether he spilled any or not. Like her mother, he was smiling.

"You don't mind?" She read ecstasy rather than dismay on their faces.

"We've been making plans and didn't want to tell you girls until we had them all worked out. It's similar." Her mother laughed. "We whisper and dream in bed. Some dreams we make come true, sometimes we fail, but this one we've landed."

Her mother and father held up their glasses, smiled into each other's eyes, and said, "Here's to retirement."

Bea bobbled her drink, some liquid trickling down her fingers.

"Don't waste it, darling," her mother said.

"Retirement?" She licked up the precious drops.

"We've been thinking about how to manage it for a while. We have small pension accounts and the house. A real estate agent approached us about the house."

"What about Lisa and Fran?"

"Your sisters are our responsibility, not yours." Her father leaned into her as he had so many times over the years, a slight nudge to comfort, to tell her he was on her side, to make a connection. "We've been working on the plan for a while. It's not fair for you to continue to take on so much of the load."

"It's never been fair," said Mamá. "Our families had the same expectations of us, so we accepted what you offered. You never complained. Not from the time you were a little girl and we asked you to look after your sisters. But your sisters don't see it that way. They're in a new country with different ways, and they claim independence for themselves."

"Are you sure this is what you want?"

"As sure as we were that having you was the right decision; the best decision we ever made. You're our baby and one of the finest people we know. Your help has made this moment possible. Time to seize life with both hands, darling. Take what you want for a change."

Bea scrubbed away tears. "I don't know what to say."

"I hope you know what to do," her mother teased.

"I'm so happy you can retire, Papá. I love you both."

"Then go and tell your friend that you're not going back to your parents, and you can afford your share of an apartment."

"It's more complicated than that."

"Does he love you?"

"I'm almost sure."

But I can ask Anna to rent me her apartment. And I can ask Casildo to stay with me. Will he? Or have I killed whatever chance we had by not telling him the truth sooner?

* * *

"Come in."

Cas opened the study door in response to his father's voice. "Have you got time for a chat?"

"Come in, come in." His father looked more relaxed than Cas had seen him in months, since before Nick Richardson. "Take a seat. I wanted to ask why you've called a family meeting."

"I've got something I need your help with, my family's help with." Cas settled onto the old chesterfield. An early purchase after a business success. Cas had stroked the leather, glorying in the fabric. His father had shared his glee. Cas had forgotten that. His dad was a tactile person, as well as a hardhead. Maybe this would be okay?

"And you wanted a few words with me first?"

"I've been wanting to talk to you for a while."

"Why haven't you?" A simple question, which shamed Cas.

"I was working up to it, but I might have misunderstood a few things. Hunt said I might have misunderstood a few things."

Cas had re-examined the facts after his conversation with Hunt. Cas didn't know the extent of the regional properties, because that was another question he'd never asked. "You've been different since Nick Richardson tried to take over The Hariri building. I've been worried. Is there anything I can do to help?"

"You helped me more than anyone else." His father's gentle smile sliced through him.

"Not true, Baba." Cas murmured the childish endearment.

"You offered me all you had. Hunter bailed me out, but not at the risk of his business or his dreams. We both understood that. Because of the nature of his business and connections, he was able to move fast, and I'll always be grateful."

"Why have you been so distant, locking yourself in here all hours of the day and night," Cas asked. Living in Maha's granny flat, eating with the family, Cas had been a witness to patterns he wouldn't otherwise have seen.

His father's brow creased. "I've always worked long hours. Maybe you've forgotten?"

"I thought you'd cut back." Cas had assumed as he'd got older, as the business had seemed secure, his father would have reduced his work schedule.

"I'm a workaholic. Occupational hazard for a lot of migrants. We have things to prove to our new countrymen as well as the families we left behind. You've all inherited the same habit. Haven't you worked two jobs at least for years?"

"Yes." Looks like his father had paid more attention to Cas's life than Cas had to his father's.

"And, I'm not always alone." His father gave a roguish wink. "Your mother is part of every plan. Just as I imagine Anna will be part of all Hunter's plans from now on. That's what I want for you."

"Actually, I've met someone, but we ended it." Saying it aloud was a gut punch, pain rippling outwards to paralyse him.

"Were you going to tell me?"

"No," Cas admitted. Beatriz deserved better than being a secret. They both deserved better. "It's complicated."

"Why?"

"Neither one of us is in a position to start a relationship."

"Why, I ask again?"

"You always said you waited until you had the money to support a wife. That's what you've been telling me for years. That was the message from my childhood."

"I exaggerated." His father raised a hand and let it fall. "It would have been easier if we'd waited until we had more money. That's another problem with being a demigod, you believed everything I said. Zahra didn't. Your sister was still a student, but she and Carlos were both sure."

"Carlos was already practising medicine. He had an income."

"You're of age, virile, you get your brains from your mum and your work ethic from me. You have a regular income. What's to stop you?"

"She's the eldest child, a second-generation migrant, although, like Maha, she wasn't born in Australia. Her parents have struggled. Her salary is needed at home." Summarising the problem made it seem more manageable. Made his solution sound reasonable.

"Did you know this before you gave me your life savings?"

His father's question forced Cas to confront a problem he hadn't had to face. Would he still have had savings if he could have freed Beatriz from her obligations?

"I wasn't seeing her then." Cas breathed easier, seeing the tension drain from his father's face.

"I'd like to meet her. What's her name?"

"You've already met her. Beatriz. Beatriz Gomez."

"Ah. Your mother's going to say I told you so. She went back and found Beatriz in the wedding photos."

"When you get to know her better, you'll love her."

"If you do, so will I. Does Hunter know about you and Beatriz?"

"Anna asked Beatriz to stay over at the apartment, Hunter asked me. We both refused, then changed our minds. We've been flatmates for a month."

"Did you meet her through Anna?"

"I've known her for about five years. We've met at work functions over the years."

"If Hunter knows about Beatriz, this isn't about telling me first. What did you want to say, son?"

"I'd forgotten your patterns. Living here, I decided that you'd withdrawn, that Nick had hurt you. Not the money, but shaken your confidence in yourself."

"In some ways, you're our most perceptive child." His father sank back into his chair. "He attacked my sons, he attacked me to get to you, to get to Hunter. I feared he was intent on driving a wedge between you and Hunter, and I was powerless to stop him. It's not a nice feeling being powerless, especially as I'm a mini demigod here at home."

Cas chuckled at the dad joke.

"I should have known better. You and Hunter breathe the same air. Sometimes, I'd swear, your hearts beat to the same rhythm. Lucky Beatriz wasn't on the scene because you'd have torn yourself apart trying to rescue all of us. I love that about you."

"I've been doing some study ..." Cas heard the front doorbell and knew his private chat with his father was nearing its end. "On property management and development. To go with my basic business degree. I planned to offer to come in alongside you, take some of the burden."

"That's a sacrifice I couldn't accept." His father was adamant. "Plus, you'd be crap at it."

"Lucky I changed my mind then." He met his father's gaze. "I thought you were disappointed in me."

"Never."

"Not even about Monique?"

"I cried," his father said. "Your mother and I cried together because we could see what she wanted. We could see the future we'd dreamed of for you slipping away. That was our disappointment. Never you. I love you, son. I loved you from the moment I knew of your existence. You, of all our children, have your jaddatee's gentle soul—a precious treasure. You also have her passion and her courage."

Tears stung the back of Cas's eyes. "Hunt told me I was wrong."

"I must thank him."

"Might as well get the rest of it out. I thought I had to be a self-made man, like you."

"You think I got here without help? Unbeknownst to me, your mother managed to get some valuable jewellery out of Saud. She worked full-time. You kids were so damn good. I didn't have the worries other parents had, and in my time of strife, you were all here."

"That makes it easier." Cas could hear steps in the corridor. "I'm here to ask for your support instead."

"What can I do?"

An imperious knock sounded at the door.

"Sounds like Mum."

"She does have her own special knock." Raed Hariri rose to his feet. "Does Hunter know what you want?" He came around the desk toward Cas.

"He knows."

"I'm glad we had this chat." His father kissed him. "Better open the door before she knocks it down.

Cas's mother stood on the other side of the door. "The dining table works better. It at least has chairs for everyone."

Cas and his father dutifully followed her into the other room, where Maha and Zahra, his second sister, were already seated. Hunter lounged against the large sideboard. Cas's mum had set a jug and water glasses on the table, ice and slices of lemon in bowls beside them. Cas stopped between his sisters, squeezed Maha's shoulder and bent to kiss Zahra's cheek. "It seems like forever since I saw you, Zaza."

"That's because you're worse than Dad when it comes to work." She softened her response with a smile. As a hospital intern, she was no slouch herself.

"How many favours did you have to call in to get off this early?" Maha asked.

"No more than you. Hunt has more control over his hours, and I guess Cas's boss can't complain if once in a while his lead artistic talent leaves at the standard time."

"I often leave at the standard time." This was an old family debate.

"Children, do we have to do this every time?" Hunter mimicked Cas's mother's voice, which made her giggle, before taking the seat beside Cas. Sisters on one side, brothers on the other with his father at the head and his mother at the foot. Cas couldn't remember when they'd settled on their seating arrangements, but it worked. The build-up of tension that had nearly overwhelmed him in the last week leaked away.

"You have the floor, Cas."

Hunter nudged Cas with his shoulder; his way of showing how much it meant to him to be part of the Hariri family.

"We're listening." Maha spoke for all of them.

"As you know we almost lost The Hariri—"

"The name of the building should go," Cas's mother interjected, throwing a hand in the air. "You only did that to prove to your grandfather that you had a name in Australia."

"The only reason we didn't lose the building was that first Casildo, then Hunter stepped in. Between you, you gave me room to manoeuvre," Raed said.

Cas stood. Interruptions and digressions were a family tradition. "Has anyone remembered I have the floor?"

"Speak then," Maha said," I've got a date."

Cas's mother and sister swivelled to stare at Maha, but

she'd won him clear air.

"I'm launching my textile printing business." He skipped the preliminaries he'd planned. "I need suitable premises and a line of credit to provide a safety net in the first two years."

"Because the first two years of a new business are the toughest?" Zahra planned to open a GP practice with her husband, and had probably already done more due diligence than Cas.

Cas had other reasons, but he wasn't sharing. Yet.

"What do you need from us?" Maha studied him. They'd always been close; she'd always been protective of him, then him and Hunt.

"Support, mostly. Dad's already paid me back the money I lent him. I've chatted to my boss, and we've negotiated a consultancy, plus I'll do some training sessions for them. So, I'll have a separate stream of income. I can sell some designs as well as run my own line."

"You offered everything you had, Cas. Your mother and I know that. We want to do more," Raed interrupted.

"We all know that," Zahra cut in, surprising Cas.

Cas had intended to tell his father everything before anyone else arrived, but maybe this was better. "I've asked Hunter to provide the premises."

There was a moment of silence, when he thought his father was offended, then Raed nodded.

"He'll be a partner," Cas finished.

"Minor," Hunter added, but his family digested the words that weren't said. Hunter had refused a partnership when Raed Hariri offered it, but had agreed to a partnership when Cas had seen sense and asked for Hunter's help.

"So, I get to supply the line of credit?" Raed studied his son.

"I'm asking you to support my plan. A line of credit would help, but I don't want to add to your financial burden."

His father rolled his eyes. "Truly, Maha did get Cas's

share of wheeling and dealing along with her own. He's as naked as a babe in the commercial property environment."

"Not funny," Maha chastised their dad.

"Your exposé of Nick Richardson had some unintended consequences for him, Hunter."

"He's not bankrupt," Hunter said. "I checked."

"He was forced to let go of some of his investments, and the market opened in unexpected ways." Raed Hariri winked.

"Which you took advantage of?" Zahra was keeping up.

"You're better off than when Nick attacked you?" Hunter asked.

"You were distracted, leaving the way open for others to take advantage."

"Her name's Anna, and I'm happy to be distracted for the rest of my life."

"That's why you need parents who pay attention." Raed gestured toward his wife. "We humbly offer ourselves in the role."

"You could give me a line of credit with no negative impact on your finances?" Cas asked.

"Will someone explain to this changeling about how property markets work when done right?" Raed smiled at his wife.

"You're not just managing?" Cas asked.

"I'm thriving."

Cas grinned. "Then can I have a line of credit, please?"

"Yes." His father looked proud of him.

"If we're setting conditions, I have another." Cas's mother surprised them all. "You're going to print your own designs?"

"With help."

Maha considered him. "Mo Husic. He's become available. Is he another partner?"

"He has. Mo will be a tenant and a supplier. He's got the right printing equipment, and he's ready to branch out."

"Without meaning to put a spanner in the works"—

Maha could write a business plan in her sleep—"who's handling your brand marketing and sales?"

"I have someone in mind," Cas confessed. "I just have to convince her to do it."

Cas's mother gave a wolf-whistle. In the sudden silence, she said, "What do you have to do to get the floor in this family?"

"You've got the floor."

"I want a new bedroom. Everything from curtains to lampshades to bed linens. I've waited years for this moment."

"You'll be first, Mum."

"I should get back to the kids." Zahra hugged him. "Good work."

"Anna's waiting for me." Hunter grinned.

"You mean waiting for a debrief."

Hunter waved a hand in the air as he headed for the door. "Whatever."

"You always said you wanted to go it alone." Maha pulled him aside when the others had left. "Is there anything else you're not telling us?"

"I love Beatriz. I want a life with her, so I'm asking for help to create the space in my life for that to be possible."

"Right choice." She hugged him.

"I don't know what I'll do if I can't convince her."

CHAPTER SEVENTEEN

Mid-afternoon Bea heard the front door open and made her way into the hall. Only two other people had keys, and Anna would have warned her. Plus, both Casildo and Anna would normally be at work.

"Casildo?" Her mouth dropped open in surprise.

"You're here? I mean, you're here mid-afternoon," he babbled.

He looked wonderful, thrusting flowers, champagne and salady things at her.

"So are you."

"You look pale, are you okay, Beatriz?"

"I've taken a few days off work." She stared at his outstretched arms.

"But, you got the promotion. Your text said Jackson was fired. Did I ever tell you you're beautiful?"

"I love you." She sagged against the wall, filling her senses with him.

"Did you mean to say that?" He stared at her.

"I'm babbling, but I've been wanting to say those words for forever. Whatever else happens, that's true."

"We're both babbling. So far, I like what I'm hearing."

He hadn't said he loved her.

"Why do you look like you've been crying?"

"Probably because I have. We're not the kind of people to rant and rage, Casildo, although I've come close." She'd never felt so helpless in her life.

"I want to shout until I'm hoarse."

"Antonio's made a counteroffer. I wanted to ask what you thought."

"That's good, isn't it?"

"I don't know what's good anymore, and I've got verbal diarrhoea. I want to tell you everything at once." She placed a hand over her racing heart. " I should start with asking why you're here."

"I brought you these." He dropped the bag of salady things on the floor and held out the flowers and champagne.

"Why?"

"Marry me." He seemed surprised by his words.

She jerked away from the wall. "I beg your pardon."

"I've had a few ideas. The first was just to give you the money." He abandoned the flowers and bottle on the hall sideboard. "But you'd have baulked at that. This is my second idea. Marry me, then it makes sense to accept half your parents' mortgage from me, because I'll be family too. We each pay half. What do you think?"

"I love you, Casildo. But I can't marry you and take your money." She wiped away a tear.

"Don't cry." He took her arm and led her toward the living room. "Hunt said you'd hate both those ideas."

"You didn't need Hunter to tell you that."

"No, I didn't. I'm not giving up the business. I've restructured. Hunt's my partner. He's providing the premises and a few other things. Turns out he had the premises. Dad's offered a line of credit for emergencies. Mo will be a tenant and do all my printing." He blurted out the entire proposal.

"Did you hear the first thing I said?" Her head was spinning with his news and hers, but he needed to understand loving him was the most important thing.

"I know you love me, Beatriz. That isn't our problem." Sinking into an armchair, he settled her on his lap. "I'm renting an apartment. Deal done. And I'm inviting you to join me."

"What do you get out of that?"

"You. And that's enough, but I don't want you angsting about it, so the quid pro quo is doing my brand management and helping me keep the books. I'm a slave driver, so you don't need to worry that you won't be pulling your weight."

"You're a miracle."

"That as well." He rested his forehead against hers. "Let me hold you for a bit. I've missed you."

She wrapped her arms around him and snuggled lower in his embrace. "I've missed you too. Why do you want to marry me?"

"Because I love you too. Everything seems less without you." He pressed his lips against her temple. "Because this is where I'm meant to be."

"I have more to tell you. My parents have sold the house."

He leaned back and met her gaze, understanding slowly replacing the confusion in his eyes.

"Contracts have been exchanged." Bea shook his shoulder slightly, relief and excitement finally seeping into her. "That's where they were the night we went to dinner. Settlement is in twelve weeks. The final three months' mortgage payments will be sorted as part of the final settlement. Effective immediately, my salary is my own."

He frowned. "You haven't made some side deal to bankroll your sisters."

"I'd already told Mamá and Papá that Fran and Lisa were on their own. Seems they've been working on this plan for a while. A real estate agent approached them. They'll get enough from the sale to buy an apartment for themselves outright, and to put a deposit on one closer to the university for Fran and Lisa to rent. My sisters have twelve weeks to find jobs."

"How do you feel?"

"Stunned. Mamá and Papá started making this move before I lost the promotion, so nothing I did triggered the sale."

"I'd say everything you've done for years made it possible."

She tugged his ear. "They saw us kissing in the car."

"I'm happy for the whole world to see us kissing in a car."

"They guessed I was in love with you."

"My mum seems to have worked it out too."

"I had my own plan," she confessed, sliding one hand into his hair. "I was going to pay the mortgage, no board and no pocket money for my sisters. I'd lined up a few hospitality shifts to get my share of rent money for an apartment, and was going to ask you to share, if you'd take me?"

"You weren't leaving me?" He pushed to his feet with her in his arms.

"Well, to be honest"—Bea linked her arms around his neck—"full-time work plus some hospitality shifts would have restricted our time together, but I decided quality was better than quantity." She pressed her mouth to his ear. "I want you in my life, Casildo. Not just the occasional work function, but in my every day. I'm only half-living without you."

His grip tightened. "Since we're sharing all our secrets, I've been designing fabrics for you."

"You don't design clothing fabrics."

"For you, I'm making an exception."

"Is that where we're going? To see your designs?" She pressed a kiss to his temple.

"We're going to share some quality time." He nudged the bedroom door open with his hip.

She giggled. "I have an idea for your company name."

"Tell me."

"Wahida."

"Jaddatee's name." His mouth split into a smile she never thought she'd see again. "That's brilliant." He lowered her feet to the floor.

"You gave me the idea." She wrapped her arms around his chest, holding tightly to banish the fear she'd had they wouldn't be able to find a way through this. "You said you and Mo emphasised unique. I looked up your jaddatee's name. It means unique, singular, rare and beautiful. It seemed right."

"It's better than right."

"I'm still punch drunk, processing, still half in the hell where I thought I'd lost you forever. I don't want you—us—making decisions because we're overdosing on happiness." She cupped his jaw with her hand. "You don't have to marry me."

"What if I want to?" he asked.

"Why?"

"Because you keep your promises. Because if you make a promise to me, I know you'll keep it. You make me feel invincible, able to leap tall buildings in a single bound."

"Mo's already taken the name Sunshine Superman." She brushed a kiss to his lips.

"More than one superhero can leap tall buildings in a single bound."

"My superhero knowledge is clearly lacking. Have you told your family?"

"I asked for their help with my business. Said I loved you, but you had family responsibilities limiting your options. They're good with family responsibilities. My dad's proud of me. But they offered to give me references if you needed any convincing."

"We don't need to rush into marriage, so long as we take our next steps together."

"Thank you, Jaddatee." He lifted her high in his arms and tossed her onto the bed.

"Have I said I love you?"

"Tell me again."

AUTHOR'S NOTE

I started this series with the theme of choosing family because your birth family might be dysfunctional, unwelcoming or even harmful to you, and I strongly believe that we can create new, bigger and different families to surround ourselves with love and support.

However, not every family is dysfunctional. Think of the mothers who drag themselves out of bed when they're sick because a child needs them, or the father who comes running when they hear you scream, the uncle or aunt who gives you a shoulder to cry on, the partner who is the other half of you.

AN ACCIDENTAL FLATMATE is about strong families who make sacrifices for the good of the whole; migrant families who weave old and new customs to make new families in new lands. Compromises take courage and love. I hope you agree that Beatriz and Casildo have both and deserve their happily-ever-after.

Be Sure To Catch The Books In The Choosing Family Series....

MASQUERADE

Fool me once...

Money won't bring LIAM QUINN'S father back, but it'll save his mother's home. A high-paying law partnership is in his sights. To win it, he needs to successfully land a project. Problem is the project requires absolute confidentiality, and he's just discovered his estranged identical twin is appearing life size on a billboard across the city. The second catch is a return to environmental law. His earlier career imploded after his lover was revealed as a mining company spy.

Researcher and soon-to-be-published romance author KATE TURNER needs a disguise. Maybe more than one. Her famous playwright father despises 'trashy' novels. Her ex-boyfriend mocked her 'dirty little secret', then stalked her when she left him. Her identical twin coaxes her into appearing on a billboard to prove she can be notorious and anonymous at the same time. No one connects the billboard model to the dowdy researcher Kate has become, and no one knows about her author pseudonym and second disguise as Ms. Sexy Romance.

Kate and Liam's lives collide when she's hired as Liam's research assistant. Liam's boss laughs off the billboard. Having doubles is the perfect cover for confidential field work.

A masquerade, a road trip, a steamy attraction, the sudden appearance of Liam's old lover, and Ms. Sexy Romance's unexpected arrival in the wrong place at the wrong time, and Liam and Kate discover the steps they took to protect their hearts might break them.

--"A Jennifer Raines romance will make you sigh in the best possible way!"-- Best Selling Author, Grace Burrowes

EXCERPT

Liam gestured to her report, open in front of him. "Simple summaries of assorted environmental disputes across Australia. That's not a lot to work with."

"Have you read my report, Mr. Quinn?" Kate emphasised his surname, annoyance at the snub for her research trumping her anxiety at exposure. She'd back her research skills against anyone in this room.

"I've scanned it." His shoulder lifted in an offhand shrug.

Arrogant moron. Another man living in an echo chamber, so sure his worldview was right not even a drone buzzing overhead would alert him to imminent attack. Was he hostile because his identical twin Niall had kept the billboard campaign secret from him? Or generally hostile to new ideas? "Then you're being deliberately offensive."

"Not yet," he answered, leaning forward—a panther preparing to spring.

Dismayed to be so attuned to his slightest movement, she stiffened her spine.

Liam had her second-guessing her defence strategy.

Until Liam, Kate had trusted that Ms. Dowdy Researcher couldn't be linked to the billboard—the final stress test to confirm no one, especially not her besuited, controlling ex-boyfriend, would recognise Ms. Dowdy as Anna Turner's twin.

QUINN, BY DESIGN

She's antiques royalty, he's relentlessly modern

Master carpenter NIALL QUINN's passion is creating bespoke furniture. Everything else comes second until his ex-fiancé ditches him when he gifts another creation to a friend, and he discovers his brother has been carrying his dead father debts. Niall's self-respect demands he pay his share. He's landed a prestigious exhibition of his work with a top gallery, possible in part because of the support of an antiques dealer who's been mentor, patron, and generous landlord. Niall's hoping the exhibition will establish his reputation and boost his bank balance.

LUCY McTAVISH's grandfather, antiques supremo Cameron (Cam) McTavish raised her. His death leaves her totally alone. Lucy drained their personal accounts to provide twenty-four-seven in-home palliative care for Cam. The thought of poverty paralyses her, a crippling reminder of life before Cam found her. Laden with debt, she plans to sell Cam's workshop to ensure his antiques emporium survives.

When the will is read, Niall Quinn holds the keys to Cam's workshop. Lucy's convinced he conned her grandpa in his last days and demands he restore antiques for her. Niall is blindsided by the bequest, but worries about yet another debt and agrees to the work.

Lucy and Niall circle each other. In sharing stories and drawing closer, Lucy figures out debt is her childhood bogeyman resurrected by Cam's death. Niall has real debts and, unaware of his exhibition, she looks for clients who'll pay him for the work she'd been demanding for free.

With the exhibition drawing closer, it's crunch time. Will Niall choose his exhibition or Lucy? Does Lucy want a man who won't share his dreams with her?

Award winning author Jennifer Raines' stories combine a love of romance with contemporary conflicts. Her writing is both relevant and heart-warming. Each story is a journey across the world. Jennifer likes to think her readers get occasional hints of the deep passion of a Nora Roberts or the unshakeable loyalty of a Grace Burrowes where love conquers loneliness, distrust and fear.

EXCERPT:

"I didn't ask for that." She made a face at the oversized sandwich he'd set in front of her.

"It's lunchtime." Niall took the chair opposite her.

Her guilty glance at her smartwatch told him she'd lost track of time, while her unfashionably baggy clothes told him eating was a faint memory. Loss of appetite was another by-product of heartache.

He'd been there too. "I hate to eat alone."

"I thought you lived alone." She cut one half of her sandwich in half and added pickles. Eating his food was another nod to politeness. Referring to his living arrangements was her opening salvo in hostilities.

"What else did your granda tell you?" Niall waited for her to swallow her first mouthful, then took a bite of his own, setting himself the task of keeping her in his kitchen long enough to finish her sandwich. Food was his currency for sympathy, although Lucy McTavish's unannounced arrival declared she wasn't here for comfort.

"Months ago, Grandpa talked about meeting a furniture restorer at an antiques auction."

"I've done the odd bit of restoration." Niall was pretty positive Cam had offered those pieces as a sop to Niall's dignity. While the profit from their sale had covered the rent, over time, Niall worked out Cam had become his patron rather than his landlord.

And wasn't that a feckin' indictment. At thirty-four, he needed an old man's patronage because his passion for making bespoke furniture had yet to deliver a decent living.

"Three pieces." She placed her left hand on his table as if drawing strength from the age and beauty of the timber. "Three pieces of furniture were delivered to McTavish's Antiques five months ago."

"Cam said they earned a good profit." Niall wrapped both hands around his Blue Italian Spode cup, watching as she raised the Flora Danica, Royal Copenhagen to her mouth; a distraction while she framed her answer. Like most of his cups, the matching saucers were lost in the mists of time.

"They did." Her chin jut signalled a full stop on McTavish profits.

"Cam said he told you about our arrangement." Niall's doubts were growing. Furniture restorer was a half-arsed description of him.

"He told me he offered you accommodation in return for restoring furniture. Three pieces of furniture over eight months gives you a higher hourly rate than a top-class hooker." The insult rolled off her tongue, the barb sinking deeper than she could have known. Unaware, she popped the last morsel of the second quarter of sandwich into her luscious, bow-shaped mouth.

BETRAYAL

They are wary of trusting, but ... passion has its own rules.

Marketing manager, ANNA TURNER promised reliable, affordable childcare to co-workers under pressure. Proud of negotiating the perfect lease for her employer, a hostile takeover of the building steals her ideal premises.

Architect and property-developer, HUNTER THOMPSON, smells betrayal on his father's breath. An old pattern, but this time his old man plans a hostile takeover of a building owned by the family who raised Hunter as a second son. Hunter out-manoeuvres his father, buying the building himself.

Attending an industry cocktail party, Anna hears Hunter say her magic word, "architect". Revealing her ideal childcare centre plan to him, Anna discovers Hunter tore up her precious lease. Anna is breathtaking in her rage. Intrigued, Hunter offers a new lease, with the opportunity to work together.

Hunter can't risk long term. Anna doesn't do hook-ups—ever. Hidden within their whirlwind romance and growing trust, secrets resurface with devastating consequences. Anna's mantra—'*I share myself, you share yourself, if you want to get into my bed*'—may not survive.

Wary strangers find passion on a shared project, until secrets from their past ambush them. Fans of Grace Burrowes stories where love conquers loneliness and fear, will fall for Jennifer Raines's heartwarming romances.

EXCERPT

"Who bought the building?" Bea prepared for her meetings with meticulous care.

"H. S. Thompson was all the managing agent would give me. Who names their child after a famous dead journalist, for Pete's sake?"

Bea held up a hand. "So, why didn't you send an apology for this shindig?"

"Antonio wanted a presence and reminded me it was my turn to come. 'Cocktail parties loosen tongues and increase personal contacts,'" Anna repeated Antonio's encouragement.

"Networking—naughty and nice?" Bea grinned. "Bet you didn't tell him you were gonna wear your *Killing Eve* dress. He's an understanding boss, but Antonio was present when you took that last dude down, and it probably wasn't what he had in mind tonight."

"I'm wearing it tonight to exorcise my rage, so I can renegotiate from a place of calm." Anna waved her hand from her head to her belly in a gesture of serenity. "But, you're right, I should go."

"On the basis that researching the buyer trumps gladhanding strangers?"

"On the basis I might bite someone's head off when I'm meant to charm. Like the guy looking this way." Anna had been aware of the guy for a while. Now, she put her hand on her friend's arm and adjusted their positions. "Make it casual, Bea. Over my shoulder, about two o'clock. The guy with the lean and hungry look." Anna's pulse raced, a lick of interest curling through her body.

"He's just looking at this stage." Bea's husky contralto oozed intrigue.

"Who is he?"

"I don't recognise him, but he wouldn't have got past security without an invite." Bea took a sip of her drink. "Mid-thirties, tall, dark, broody rather than handsome, and on his own. He's perfected the stiff-backed, imperious, don't-mess-with-me look. Out of place in a crowd like this. Do you want me to find out?"

"Yes." Anna sipped her icy mineral water and waited a heartbeat. "No."

"Well, that's clear." Bea flashed her dimples.

A JUST MAN

When past and present collide, a passionate attraction detonates in this enemies to lovers romance from award winning author, Jennifer Raines. Grab a copy today!

No matter where you run, the past will find you...

Kelly needs to enhance her resume. Why else would she accept a placement in Tullamore facing her phobia about country towns? Years ago, a rookie cop humiliated her during an illegal strip search. Problem is, that former cop is now the deputy principal of her new high school and her boss. Sharing a house, a commute, and now an investigation to unravel a series of disasters that look like sabotage, Kelly takes the previously unthinkable step from enemies to allies to lovers.

Taking a job as deputy principal to uncover suspected corruption at the school, Mick plans to use the appointment as a stepping stone to principal of his own school. Then Kelly, his biggest mistake in his short time on the force, walks through his door. Given the chance to make amends brings peace for both, until Kelly is caught in the crosshairs of his investigation. Protecting her is his only goal.

Jennifer's books have elements of Emily Henry, where characters are the result of layer upon layer of experiences and emotions, where self-doubt becomes our wound. Jennifer draws on a long history of romance writers where passion flares and love conquers loneliness, distrust and fear.

EXCERPT:
"I've called the cops." A guy yelled from the direction of the apartments. "I've had it with you trashing the place and stealing my gear."

Shit!

Furious with herself, Kelly assessed the situation. The guy was probably yelling at the hoodies. Had he seen her? Could she sit it out?

The boys scrambled out of the yard, the smash of upturned bins and broken bottles marking their escape. A siren sounded nearby, brakes squealed, then car doors slammed.

Don't open the door.

Kelly tightened her hold on the post.

The guy who'd called the cops yelled out, "I reckon someone's in the garage."

Damn!

Her skin iced. Someone dragged a door open, the sound scraping against her nerves. A large torch flicked on, flooding the front of the garage with light. The holder used high beam to scan the four corners, then slowly played the light up the walls, along the roof joists. The beam skated over her, then backtracked to spotlight her. She froze, her muscles stretched painfully tight. Her mind played out the scene to come.

"Come on down, girlie." Impossible to make out the face behind the voice, but the tone and the emphasis on "girlie" were familiar tells. Tried, judged and found guilty. This burly cop was keen on punishment.

His offsider hoisted a ladder she'd missed against the side wall, slapping it against the beam next to her. It bounced, the echo shuddering through her.

"You're under arrest," top cop roared. "Come down by yourself, or I might have to tell my boy to come up and get you."

"What's the charge?" Kelly's mouth went dry.

She knew her rights. She also knew they were worth zilch in a small town where rogue police could make their own rules. Lack of official oversight was explicit permission for some tin-pot dictators. Her caramel skin tones, dark hair and eyes complicated the equation.

"Trespassing on private property. Vandalism and intent to injure."

She started down the ladder, the unsteadiness in her legs pissing her off. She faced him, head high. "Can I ask you your name, Officer?"

"Senior Sergeant George Hogan." He loomed over her. "What's yours?"

Welcome to bumfuck, as they say in the classics.

"Kelly Manners."

Available now in Ebook and Print- At all Major Book Retailers

ABOUT THE AUTHOR

Australian Jennifer Raines writes contemporary romances set mainly, but not exclusively, in Australia—think Malta, Finland, New Zealand or ? A dreamer and an optimist, her stories are a delicious cocktail of passion, mutual respect and loyalty because she still believes in happily-ever-afters.

Jennifer fell in love with romance as a teenager. Starting with historical romance. Everything in the school library and then a personal treasured collection of Georgette Heyer, hard copies, paperbacks and eBooks. Comfort food, she calls them, like Vegemite toast, for those times when she feels low. Her library of comfort food has grown over the years but Georgette Heyer was an early star, under the blankets after lights out using a torch.

Jennifer is a member of Romance Writers of Australia. Three times a finalist in the Emerald competition, including in 2017 (*Common Cause*, renamed *Lela's Choice*), 2018 (*Taylor's*

Law) and 2022 (*Quinn, by design* – Choosing Family Book 2). She's a member of Romance Writers of New Zealand, winning the Pacific Hearts competition twice, including in 2019 with *Grace Under Fire*, the sequel to *Taylor's Law*. She's also a member of Romance Writers of America and has been a finalist in chapter competitions in 2019, 2020 and 2021 (*Taylor's Law*). Jennifer won the contemporary romance section in the 2020 Orange Rose Contest for *Planting Hope* and was second overall. Jennifer values competitions for the constructive, honest, not always comfortable feedback they provide.

In 2023 *Taylor's Law* placed second in the Romance Writers of New Zealand Koru Best First Book

Jennifer loves those days when words flow and the joy of writing makes the hard slog worthwhile. She's always made up stories about strangers in the street, in a café or strolling through an airport terminal; finding inspiration in snippets of conversations, news items and the sheer puzzle of human interactions.

Jennifer lives in inner-city Sydney, Australia, with the requisite number of partners (1) and animals (2). Her desk overlooks a park which nourishes her soul when she raises her head from her keyboard. She gets some of her best ideas during long yin yoga poses or walking—anywhere. While Jennifer adores historical romance, she chose to write contemporary because she thought (wrongly) it needed less research while she was holding down a full-time job.

You can find out more about Jennifer and her writing at https://jenniferrainesauthor.com   or   via https://www.facebook.com/jenniferrainesauthor

Or https://www.instagram.com/romanceauthorjen/

Her book(s) are available through major providers.